Presented to

____

from

____

____

Date ________________________

Through-the-Year Stories

Through-the-Year Stories

Stories by V. Gilbert Beers
Illustrations by Samuel J. Butcher

BAKER BOOK HOUSE
Grand Rapids, Michigan 49516

This special paperback edition issued 1995 by
Baker Books
a division of Baker Book House Company
P.O. Box 6287, Grand Rapids, Michigan 49516-6287

ISBN: 0-8010-4104-X

Printed in the United States of America

Contents

July

August

September

Letter to Parents

Growing up on an Illinois grain farm offered me a carousel of the four seasons, and a smorgasbord of all that went with them. Farm life meant outdoor life much of the time and that meant participating with autumn leaves, shocks of corn, thunderstorms, falling snowflakes, frosty designs on the old farmhouse windows, the first buds on the trees in the spring, summer gardening, and hundreds of other signs of the wonders of God's special through-the-year fingerprints and footprints on our world.

The seasons and their unique wonders meant so much to me, and to my wife, Arlie, that they became the focal point of many of our activities with our five growing children. Some of our happiest memories with our children are those associated with the wind blowing in the trees, discovering wildflowers in the woods, finding animal shapes in puffy white summer clouds, building snowmen, and raking autumn leaves. Seasonal pictures always found their places around our house, hanging on walls, adorning the refrigerator door and almost any place the children could hang them. Is it surprising that our grandchildren are now enjoying these same wonders?

With the advent of television many of our children are losing their appreciation for God's created wonders. If this book serves as an appetizer for you and your children to participate in seasonal wonders, it will have served you well. But while you find affinity with your children and creation, I trust also that you, and they, will find affinity with the Creator.

V. Gilbert Beers

January

Something New

There's something new
around our house;
It's not a cat,
it's not a mouse.

It's nothing that
my mother hid,
So don't try lifting
every lid.

And Dad says, "No,
I didn't hide
A thing for you
to find outside."

Oh, now I think I'm very near!
I found we have a *BRAND NEW YEAR!*

January

Betty B. wants to be
Outside skating with you and me.

Christopher C. wants to see
How fast his sled slides when it's slippery.

Donna D. wants to be free
To help Mom take down
the Christmas tree.

Everett E. said to me,
"I'd rather say HAPPY NEW YEAR
To the other three."

It's Only a Piece of Wood

It's only a piece of wood. That's what I thought when I carried an armload of wood into our house. Then I remembered.

Since I was little we had a big tree in our back yard. Dad built a tree house in it. Have you ever played in a tree house? You know how much fun we had. When friends came, we played games and had parties in our tree house. But we could not have a tree house without a big tree, could we?

Sometimes we sat under this big tree and watched the wind blow its leaves. It's fun to watch the green leaves blow, isn't it? We talked about the wind. Where did it come from? Where did it go? Who sent it? Was it having fun playing in our big tree? Maybe it would like to play with us in our tree house.

Birds hopped around the branches of our big tree. Sometimes they built a nest on a branch. Squirrels played on the branches of the big tree, too. It was fun to watch them play.

One day a big storm came. Lightning flashed. Thunder rolled across the sky like a bowling ball rumbling across the clouds. The wind blew so hard and the branches were bent so low we thought the big tree would fall. But it didn't. It stood tall and straight, like a strong giant. The next day we played in our tree house again.

When fall came the leaves on the big tree began to change color. You should have seen the beautiful colors. Some leaves were red. Others were yellow. And some were orange and yellow and red. Dad said the tree was changing its clothes before it went to sleep for winter.

But something awful happened. The old tree died. There was nothing we could do to help it. I guess it just got too old.

I cried when some men tore down our wonderful tree house. I cried again when they cut down the old tree.

Then men cut the old tree into little pieces. I'm carrying some of them inside.

It's only a piece of wood. But Dad says it's really much more than that.

He's carving a beautiful wooden duck from a piece of the old tree. He thinks the old tree would be glad that something beautiful can be made with its wood. He says the wood could make tables or chairs or other wonderful things. Maybe I'll pick out a special piece and ask Dad to show me how to carve a tiny canoe.

This winter our family will eat together and play together by our wood-burning stove. We will be thankful that wood from the old tree keeps us warm.

I think the old tree would be glad it can do that, too.

It's only a piece of wood.

But it's much more than that.

Can you think of other things that could be made from that old tree? Find some wooden things in your house. When you do, don't forget to think about the Person who made the trees and helped them grow. You may even want to say "thank you!"

My Snowfriend

Suppose you and I could make a very best friend. We might make this friend from boards or bricks or gadgets or widgets. Or we might even make this friend from snow. That's it! We'll make a snowfriend.

What kind of friend should we make? What kind of friend would be just right for us? Have you ever thought about this?

I want a friend who is bigger and meaner than any other kid on the block. No one will bully this new friend. If I need someone to chase away kids that pick on me, I will tell my bigger and meaner friend. He will certainly not let those kids pick on me. He will teach them a lesson they will not forget.

What did you say? This is not such a good idea? What if my bigger and meaner friend is not always friendly with me? What if he helps the other big kids pick on me?

I suppose you're right. No, we must not make a bigger and meaner friend. He may not be a good friend at all.

You say you want a friend who has lots of other friends. She is very popular. Everyone likes this friend. Whenever the kids choose teammates for a game, she is the first one chosen. Whenever we have a school play, she gets the best part. She's pretty and smart, the very best girl on the block.

But listen to what I am saying. This is not such a good idea! If she is that popular, she may not spend much time with you. If you ask her to come over to play, she may say, "I'm sorry, you will have to make an appointment. The only time I have left is next Tuesday at four in the afternoon."

You think I'm right? Of course I am. No, we must not make a very popular friend like that. She may not be a good friend at all.

How would you like a friend who has lots and lots of money? Whenever we want an ice cream cone, he will buy it for us. Whenever we want to go to the candy store or circus, he will have the money to take us. Don't you think that's a good idea?

You don't? What are you saying? You think we might ask our friend for too many things? I suppose you are right. If we think of money all the time, we'll stop thinking of all the fun things we can do without money. We could become greedy and piggy. We may even think we don't need God's help. Then who will want to be our friend?

Let's think about this a little more. If we could make our own friend, what kind of friend would really be best?

What did you say? I think you're right! Let's make a friend just like us.

GLUE

Don't you think we will have lots and lots of fun together with this special new snow-friend? I do.

A Ride on My Sled

Will you go for a ride on my bright new
    sled?
  You'll like it, I guarantee.
We'll glide like a ship with wind-filled sails,
  in snowy woods on winding trails.
We'll laugh and sing about everything,
  as we ride, just you and me.

I'll ride with you on your bright new sled.
  I'll like it, I can see.
But I have a friend I must bring along,
  perhaps she'll help, she's really strong.
We'll laugh and sing about everything,
  just you and me . . . and she.

Will you go for a ride on my bright new
    sled?
  I guess it's okay for three.
We'll sail like a plane among clouds of
    snow,
  going wherever we want to go.
We'll laugh and sing about everything,
  just you and me . . . and she.

I'll ride with you on your bright new sled.
  I'm glad there's room for three.
But if three is okay, what about four?
  I know you won't mind if I bring some
    more.
We'll laugh and sing about everything,
  as they ride with you and me.

Will you go for a ride on my bright new
    sled?

It will be crowded, I can see.
But tell your friends to come along
and bring with them a happy song.
We'll laugh and sing about everything,
our friends and you and me.

I LOVE YOU
Piggy BANK
HOME MADE
VALENTINES
WHILE YOU WAIT
JEST 5¢

February

A Heart Fixer-Upper

No one cared when her friends teased
her,
when one of them said,
"I am not your friend!"
That's what Jennifer thought
when she cried at school.
She was sure that her friends
weren't friends at all.

Jennifer thought her heart would break.
She needed someone,
a heart fixer-upper,
for her heart felt like it was cut or bruised.

No one cared when a bully
got mean,
when he picked on a
little kid
who couldn't fight back.
That's what Jennifer
thought
when she cried at
school.
She was sure
there was no one
to make things right.
She felt that her heart was hurting inside.
Jennifer needed someone,
a heart fixer-upper,
for her heart felt like it was cut or bruised.

No one cared when her best friend cried,
when she said that her dad had run away.
That's what Jennifer thought
when she cried at school.

SamB

She was sure that no one
could help her friend.
She felt there was no one
who hurt for her friend.
Jennifer needed someone,
a heart fixer-upper,
for her heart felt like it was cut or bruised.

No one cared when
her brother wouldn't play,
when Mom and Dad were too busy.
That's what Jennifer thought
when she cried at home.
She was sure that no one knew
the pain she felt.
She thought that other things
were much more important.
Jennifer needed someone,
a heart fixer-upper,
for her heart felt like it was
cut or bruised.

No one cared when her
kitty got sick,

when she stayed up late
to watch over her.
That's what Jennifer thought
when she cried at home.
She was sure that no one knew
how lonely she felt.
She thought that other things
always came first.
Jennifer needed someone,
a heart fixer-upper,
for her heart felt like it was cut or bruised.

Then Jennifer told a wise friend,
a heart fixer-upper.
He brought his first-aid kit
and he heard what her heart was
saying.
He saw that it was hurt
and needed to be fixed.
"I have a prescription," he said to Jennifer.
So he wrote his prescription
on a little piece of paper.
Now that Jennifer knew
someone else cared
when her heart felt cut or bruised,

she could follow his prescription
    to help her hurting heart.

This prescription sent Jennifer
    to see her mother.
And it said she should tell Mother
    exactly how she felt.
Mother listened to Jennifer
    and knew her heart was hurting.

And do you know
    what happened that day?
Mother said some special words
    that helped her broken heart.
And she put her arms around Jennifer
    and hugged her tight.
Then Jennifer knew
    that someone else cared.

She had found
        another fixer-upper
        to help her heart,
for Mother healed her heart
    from feeling cut and bruised.

"I have a prescription also,"
Mother said to Jennifer.
Then she wrote it down
on a little piece of paper.
Then Jennifer did what this
new prescription said.
She went to her room
and began to pray.
She talked with God
and told him how she
felt.

Jennifer knew for sure
that Someone else
cared.
She knew that she
had found
a special Someone,
another fixer-upper
who would always
help her heart.
God healed her heart
from feeling cut
and bruised.

A Dozen or More Hearts

"I'll make a valentine for Dad," said Laura, on February 14. "He's a special dad, so I want to make a valentine that tells him how special he really is."

Laura found red construction paper. She found scissors and a pen. She brought all these things to the dinette table and sat down to work.

Laura smiled as she cut the construction paper into a big red heart.

"Wait until Dad sees this!" she said. She could see him now in her mind. He would be so happy when he read what she would write on this heart.

But what should she write?

"I know," said Laura. "I will write what I like best about him. But what do I like best about Dad?"

Laura began to think. "Dad plays games with me," she said. "That's special. He also takes me on trips. And he reads to me."

Laura kept on thinking about things she liked best about Dad. Soon she had a long list. She did not have just one thing she liked best about Dad. She had fourteen.

"That's a dozen!" Laura whispered. "No! That's more than a dozen! I can't write all of these things on this one heart."

Laura read the list again. Which one special thing did she want to write on the heart?

But they were all special. She really liked every one of these things about Dad. She liked each one as much as the others. How could she choose only one from the dozen or more special things?

Then Laura had a good idea. She began to cut more red hearts from the construction paper. Before long she had fourteen red hearts.

Laura wrote one special message on each heart. Each one told Dad something she liked best about him.

Laura strung the fourteen hearts on a long string. Just as she finished, her father walked into the room.

"Having fun?" he asked.

"Happy Valentine's Day!" said Laura. Then she gave her dozen or more hearts to Dad.

Don't you think Dad had fun reading what Laura wrote on those dozen or more hearts?

I Don't Know What to Say

I want to write a little note
to a very special person.
But I don't know what to say.

I want to tell this special person
how very special she is.
But I don't know what to say.

I want to tell this special person
how thankful I am that she washes
my clothes and irons them.
But I don't know what to say.

I want to tell this special person
how much I appreciate all the good
meals she cooks for me.
But I don't know what to say.

I want to tell this special person
how much fun it is when we go shop-
ping or do things together.
But I don't know what to say.

I want to tell this special person
how glad I am that she comes
to all my school programs and things.
But I don't know what to say.

I want to tell this special person
that she has given me so many
things and I just want to say something wonderful about her.
But I don't know what to say.

I want to say a hundred thank yous
and a thousand nice things
to this special person.
But I don't know what to say.

I want to tell this special person
that I want to be just like her
when I grow up.
But I don't know what to say.

I guess you know by now
that I'm talking about you,
Mother dear.
Would it be okay if I just tell you that
I LOVE YOU
today, Valentine's Day,
and every other day too?

Love is Kind
WELCOME FRIENDS
OUR SPECIALS
HOLY BIBLE
LOVE
JOY

A New Way to Say "I Love You"

The snow had been falling an hour or
more
when Tom remembered to go to the store.
Do you have one chore—
or maybe even more?

Does Mother ever ask you to go to the
store?
Does she ask you for one chore
or even one more?

Tom's mother had not
asked Tom to do more,
but only one chore,
to go to the store.
So that's where Tom was going
when he went out the front door.

But sometimes things happen
when we start on a trip
Things happen as fast as a slip of the lip!
Things happened to Tom
as he started to skip.
He skipped
and he slipped
and something went RIP!!

Now a rip in the wrong place
can stop the best trip.
That's what happened to Tom
when his pants went RIP!

Now Tom's pants already
had
plenty of patches.
You might even say they
had
batches of patches.
But now Tom needed one
more patch
and he didn't care
if it would mix or match.

He needed someone
to attach a patch
to his pants,
already covered
with batches of patches.

But who could solve
Tom's troubles today—
so he could finish his
chore
and come home to play?

Who could patch
his ripped pants the way

his mother would do
if she weren't away?

Who could put on a patch that was okay?

And who could do it on this special day?

Today is a day called Valentine's Day.

Now look who is coming
with needle and thread.
Since Mother's not home,
here comes sister instead.
And Sis has a patch
that's a pink shade of red.
Sis sews on her patch as
Tom turns his head
and watches Sis sew
with her needle and thread.

Tom's trousers will soon be as good as
new.
(Though Tom wished his pink patch
was gray, green, or blue.)
But Tom needed a patch

so a pink patch will do,
cause his pants without patches
exposes the wrong view.

Then too, Tom also knew,
that when Sis is through,
her pink patch on Valentine's Day says,
"I LOVE YOU."

March

If I Could Make the Clouds

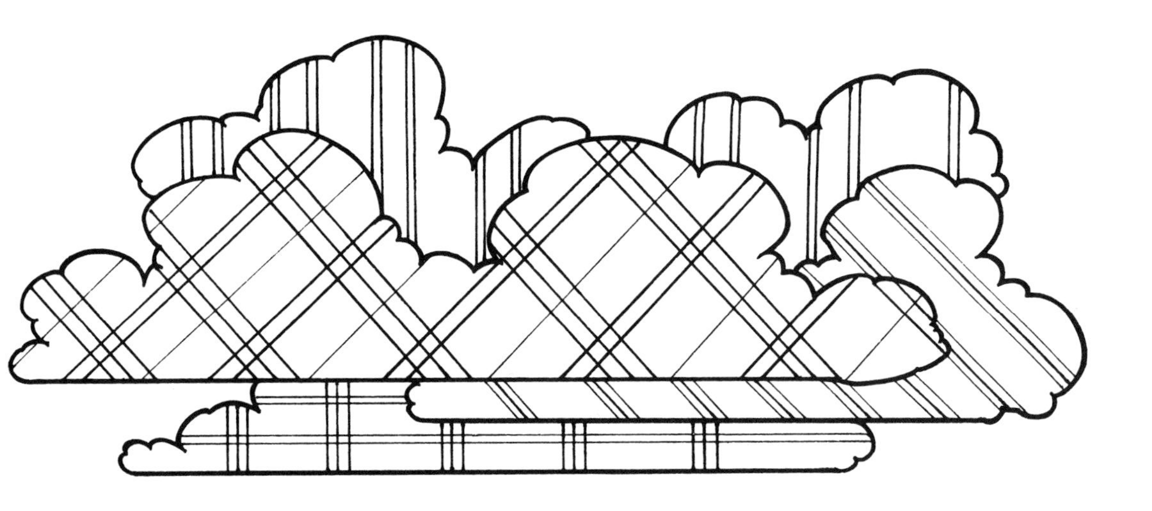

I wonder why God made clouds the way he did. Have you ever looked up into the sky in March and wondered that too?

Why did he make them look like white cotton? I think I would have made some look like my plaid winter shirt. Each cloud would be a different kind of plaid. And each one would be a different color.

Perhaps a few with stripes would be nice too! I would make stripes of different colors. Some stripes would be wide. Some would be not so wide.

Just to be different, some clouds could have dots on them. I would have red dots,

green dots, and purple ones, too. Maybe we would add some blue dots and pink dots.

Think how exciting the sky would be then!

Now that I think about it, why not make some clouds like rainbows? You know, paint lots of colors in big arches. You like rainbows, don't you?

Don't you wish I had made the clouds? The sky is getting full of color, isn't it?

Sometimes I like to watch the neon signs when we go downtown. Why not do that to the clouds? You know, light them up. Clouds are pretty during the daytime, but think how much prettier they would be at night if they were shining.

I'm wondering. Why does God make clouds from puffy white fog? Why not make some of them from bricks or boards or stones? Or some could be glass with gold frames around them.

Let's see. Is there anything else we could do with the clouds? Maybe we should stop and look at what's up in the sky with all these changes.

Oh! I didn't know I had made so many different kinds of designs up there. The sky really is a little bright. I guess there's too much color. Perhaps it's just not put together right. It's really sort of ugly, too. I don't think I like what I've done. Do you?

I guess God knew what he was doing when he made the clouds the way he did. What do you think?

The Seas of Wind

Christopher watched the clouds in the sky,
riding like ships on the seas of wind.
They were puffy white ships, sailing up high,
looking for adventure on the seas of wind.

"Where are you going?" Christopher
called to them.
"Where are you headed on the seas of
wind?"
But the cloud ship captains
were silent that day.
No one would whisper where they were
going.
No one would tell why they were sailing.
No one would send
one word for an answer.

The cloud ships were sailing
on a great adventure.
They were looking for excitement
on the seas of wind.

But where they were going was a secret.
No one would know,
not even Christopher.
Not even Christopher
would know their secret,
though he watched so carefully.

Not even Christopher
would know
where they were sailing.

They were sailing in silence
on the seas of wind.
They were sailing in silence, so far away.

"Do these ships have captains?"
Christopher whispered to himself.
"Is there someone to guide them
on the great adventure?
Is there someone to guide them
on the seas of wind?"

Soon Christopher sailed
his kite in the sky.
It sailed like a ship on the seas of wind.
It was a bright-colored ship,
sailing that day on a great adventure.
"Up to the clouds," Christopher commanded.

Then he let out more string
and the ship sailed higher,
up and away on the seas of wind.

"Stop for a while!"
Christopher commanded.

Then he tugged on the string
and the bright-colored ship
dropped anchor into
the seas of wind.

"Come this way,"
Captain Chris commanded.
When he pulled on the string,
the ship sailed toward him.
It sailed on command
of its earthbound captain
As it sailed that day
on the seas of wind.

Christopher looked at the string
in his hand.
He looked again at the kite in the sky,
the bright-colored ship
on the seas of wind.

He was captain of this ship
and he commanded its path.
With a string he
showed it where to go
sailing on the seas of wind.

So he held his string tightly
and sent his ship sailing.
It could almost touch a white puffy cloud.
Could the two ships meet
on the seas of wind,
the bright-colored ship
commanded by Christopher
and the white puffy cloud ship
on its great sea adventure?

Christopher watched
as the clouds sailed away,
sailing like ships
on the seas of wind.

The puffy white clouds,
sailing that day,
were looking for adventure
in a land far away.
Then he looked at his bright kite
on the same windy seas,
sailing like a ship and looking
for adventure.

He looked at the string,
one end in his hand,
the other stretching to the kite.

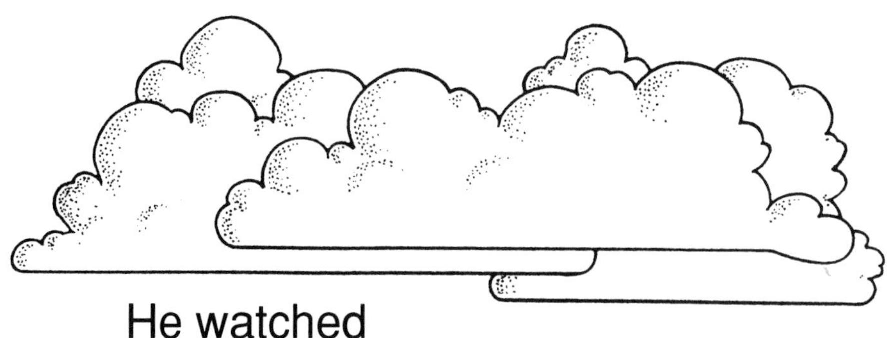

He watched
as he guided his little kite ship,
sailing away
on the seas of wind.

"The puffy white cloud ships
have a Captain, too,
a Captain to guide them
on the seas of wind,"
Christopher said as the ships sailed
above him.

Then he whispered "thank you"
to the unseen Captain,
he whispered a prayer
for guiding these ships.
And he also said "thanks"
for guiding him too,
as he dreamed of adventures
on the seas of wind.

Spilled Trouble

There was once a mom something like your mom or my mom. Of course, she wasn't exactly like our moms. No two people are exactly alike.

This mom liked to keep the house clean and neat all the time. Her kids said she even tried to keep it clean when they were playing. (That's not easy, is it?) They also said their clean-up mom told them to pick up their things before they threw them down. Do you think she really did that? She probably didn't. But you know how it seems when you want to play with a dozen toys at the same time. Who wants to stop to clean up the house then?

This mom was also a fix-up and paint-up parent. Her kids said she always carried a screwdriver in one hand or a paintbrush in the other. She didn't really do that. But you know how it seems when you're a kid. Most of us would rather play than tighten a screw or paint a door, wouldn't we?

When spring-cleaning time came the kids wanted to hide. They said their mom would probably paint *them* if they didn't get out of the way. She wouldn't really do that. But sometimes we think things are worse than they really are.

One spring-cleaning day this mom got out a can of paint. She brought the stepladder from the garage. And she found some paintbrushes. You know what she started to do, don't you? But she did not get to paint even one door.

Look at the picture to see what happened! That's enough to make anyone cry.

One of this mom's kids saw the whole thing happen. So did a couple of the neighbor kids. They all wondered what this mom would do now.

"My mom would yell a blue streak!" said one of the neighbor kids.

"My mom would sit down and cry all day," said the

other neighbor kid. "What do you think *your* mom will do?"

"Shhh," said this mom's kid. "Let's wait and see."

(While you're waiting, you might ask what you would do.) Well, here is what this mom did. She bowed her head. Then she softly said,

Dear God, I want to cry
and I want to say
some mean words.
But I don't think you want me to do
either one.
Please help me.

Amen.

Then this mom cleaned up the whole mess. She didn't say anything mean. And she didn't even cry. Well, maybe there was a tiny tear or two, but she didn't sit in the corner and cry all day.

Do you suppose this mom's prayer really did help her? You might remember that the next time something messy happens to you.

RED
BLUE

I'm Looking for a Friend

I'm looking for a friend today,
  A friend who'll never stay away.
I want one friend, or maybe two,
  But I want a friend who's just like you.

I'm looking for a friend, you see,
A friend who needs someone like me.

I want this friend, I really do,
  But I want a friend who's just like you.

I'm looking for a friend sincere,
  A friend who'll always bring good cheer.
I want a friend who wants me too,
  But I want a friend who's just like you.

I'm looking for a friend who's good,
  Who'll do the things a kind friend
    should.
I want a friend who's happy too,
  But I want a friend who's just like you.

I'm looking for a loving friend,
  Who will not let our friendship end.
I want a friend who's always true,
  I think I've found my friend—IT'S YOU!

Nobody Loves Me!

Have you ever said what Little Lamb said
When he stumbled and fell and banged
up his head?
"Nobody loves me!" that's what he said.
Then he cried when he felt the big knot
on his head.

"Nobody loves me! Nobody cares!"
Little Lamb grumbled when he tumbled downstairs.
Later he stumbled over a root,
And a very sharp thorn stuck in his foot.

Before he could cry, a gaggle of geese
Honked and chased him and pecked at his fleece.
And then a big bull, an obnoxious fellow,
Bellowed a horrendous, earthshaking bellow.

This bull chased the lamb, snorting and puffing,
Till it looked like he'd knock out the scared lamb's stuffing.
So now don't you know, now don't you see
Why Little Lamb said, "Nobody loves me"?

I'm sure you'll admit, I'm sure you'll agree
That Lamb had a right to say, "No one loves me!"
And maybe, just maybe, that's what you'll say
When you get into trouble sometime later today.

But look! There is someone who heard the lamb say
What he said when his troubles fell on him today.
Now what do you think that poor lamb will do
When the shepherd says softly, "I love you!"

Do you ever cry, “Nobody loves me”?
And you sob so hard you can’t even see?
Whenever you do, I hope you will say,
“There’s a Shepherd beside me who loves me each day.”

April

Sunshine and Raindrops

"I'm tired of snow," said Amy. "I wish it would never snow again."

"Never?" asked Father. "That's a long time. Do you remember the fun things you did in the snow this winter?"

Amy thought about the winter snow. "I really did have fun sliding down the hill on my sled," she said. "And we made this neat snowman and threw snowballs."

"And we counted snowflakes on your coat," said Father.

"I guess I really do like snow," said Amy. "But now I just want the sun to shine all the time."

"Always?" asked Father. "That's a lot of time for the sun to shine."

The next day Amy got her wish. The spring sun began to shine. Amy ran outside to play. She had so much fun playing outside. The sunshine was so nice and warm.

The sun shined all day. It shined all the next day too. And it shined for many days after that. Amy grew tired of nothing but bright sunshine.

"I guess I really don't want the sun to shine all the time," said Amy. "It would be nice to have some April showers. Then I could use my new umbrella. I wish it would rain all the time now."

"All the time?" asked Father. "That's a lot

of rain. But you do have a nice umbrella. I know you will have fun with it."

The next day Amy got her wish. Dark clouds raced across the sky. Raindrops began to fall. Amy was so happy. She ran outside with her new umbrella. She had so much fun. Her umbrella kept her quite dry while she watched the raindrops splash in the puddles. But of course she couldn't stay outside in the rain all day, could she?

It rained all that day. It also rained all the next day. Then it rained every day for several days.

"I'm tired of all this rain," said Amy finally. "I wish it would do something else. I wish it would never rain again. I would rather have snow than all this rain."

Father smiled. "But you said you never wanted snow again," said Father.

Amy looked up at Father. "I did say that, didn't I?" she said.

"You also said you would like sunshine all the time and rain all the time," Father said with a chuckle. "Or did you say you wished that it would never rain again? Would you

rather have sunshine all the time—or not at all? Or would you rather have raindrops always—or not at all?"

"What if we had a little of each?" Amy asked. "That would be better than always or never."

"So what would you like God to send now?" Father asked.

"Sunshine and raindrops," said Amy.

"Always or never?" Father asked.

"Whatever he thinks is best," said Amy.

Where Do Raindrops Come From?

Where do raindrops come from?
What is there way up high?
Does God have a garden hose
Sprinkling the April sky?

Where does lightning come from?
What is God trying to see?
Does he have a super flashlight
That he shines on you and me?

Where does thunder come from?
And why is it so loud?
Does God have a giant bowling ball
That he rolls from cloud to cloud?

Where do storm clouds come from
That bring us April rain?
Are these the shepherd's woolly sheep
That he sends past my window pane?

The Perfect Birthday Cake

"Happy birthday, Mother," said Jerry. "I'm going to make the perfect cake for you today." He imagined the yummy looking cake he would give her.

Mother smiled when she heard that. Would your mother smile if you said you were going to make a perfect birthday cake for her?

"What do you put into angel food cake?" Jerry asked.

"Do you want to make it from a cake mix or from scratch?" asked Mother.

Jerry wasn't sure what scratch was. But it sounded like it would make a more perfect cake than an old box mix.

"You'll need cake flour, baking powder, eggs, salt, sugar, and vanilla," said Mother. "May I help you?"

"No, thanks," said Jerry. "I want to do it all by myself."

Mother didn't say, "You can't do that." She didn't even say, "You shouldn't do that." She got out her favorite angel cake recipe and gave it to Jerry.

Then Mother quietly left the room.

Jerry whistled as he looked for the things to make the cake. When he found the flour and eggs he put them on the kitchen counter. Before long he also had sugar and salt and vanilla.

Jerry dumped some flour into a mixing bowl. He broke the eggs and dumped those into the flour. Then he poured in some vanilla and sprinkled a little bit of baking powder, some salt, and sugar into the bowl.

Jerry wondered how a perfect cake could come from such a gooey, lumpy mess. But he kept on whistling as he took a big spoon and stirred the gooey, lumpy mess as hard as he could. He stirred and stirred. Some of the lumps disappeared but it was still a gooey mess.

By this time Jerry wondered if maybe Mother shouldn't help him. But he still wanted to do it all by himself.

Jerry poured the gooey mess into a big cake pan. Then he popped the pan into the oven.

Just then Jerry's sister Terry came into the kitchen with their puppy FiFi.

"Whatcha doing?" she asked.

"Making a perfect birthday cake for Mother," said Jerry.

"Looks more like you're making a perfect mess," said Terry.

Jerry didn't think that was very funny. But he opened the oven door and showed Terry the cake. It certainly was a strange looking mess.

"Well, it doesn't look perfect to me," said Terry.

"Maybe it has baked too long," said Jerry. "It's been in there at least fifty minutes."

Jerry put on some padded gloves he had seen Mother use. Then he pulled out his perfect cake and dumped it onto a plate.

The cake sprawled into a mess on the plate. One side was done in spots, another

side sagged like it was too tired to stand up and be a cake. Jerry quickly stuck some birthday candles on the cake and showed it to FiFi. She thought it looked great. But Terry laughed.

"Yuk!" said Terry. "Is that a cake?"

Just then Mother walked into the kitchen. "Happy Birthday, Mother," said Jerry.

Mother almost laughed. But she didn't.

"I'm afraid it's not a perfect cake," said Jerry. "I'm afraid it's not even a good cake."

"Must be something wrong with the recipe," said Mother.

"Recipe?" said Jerry. "Oh, no! I forgot to follow the recipe! That's why it's a mess."

"I guess that's what happens to our lives when we forget to follow what God tells us, isn't it?" Terry asked.

"That's right," said Mother. "Maybe this isn't a perfect birthday cake. But I think it's a good reminder. When we think about this cake we'll remember that we need to follow a recipe or directions. It will help us remember to do exactly what God tells us. This certainly is a very special cake after all!"

May

The Very Best Painting

When Jason went by,
the flowers bowed low
and he bowed back to them.

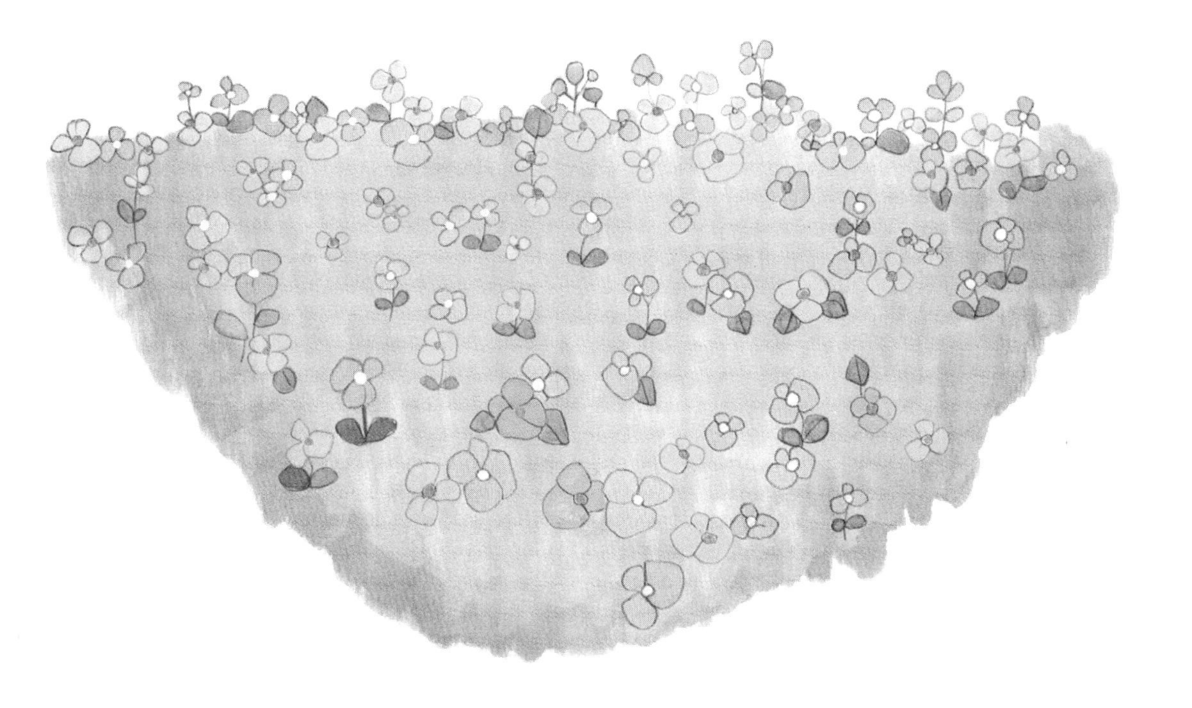

They seemed to smile
so he smiled, too.
The flowers bowed low
with the wind and said,
"Look at me!
Look at me!
Look at me!"

"I'll paint a flower
that's better than the real thing,"
Jason whispered,
much too loud.

"You flowers in the field will say,
'I wish I could look that good today.
I wish I could be like Jason's flower.
No other flower can be that way.'"

So Jason took out his paints and easel.
He waved his brushes in the air.
The masterpiece began!

He painted fast and furiously,
painting a flower
to be better than a flower:
Or so he thought it would be.

But the more he painted,
the more he frowned
And the flowers in the field looked away.
Reds and yellows,
greens and blues,
all went on his paper.
Some went this way, some went that.
But all went the way his brushes went.
There was nothing else they could do.

Now Jason's frown got even bigger.

He looked at the paints
he had used that day.
He looked at the reds
and greens
and yellows
and blues.
"This flower I made isn't better at all,"
Jason said that day.
"It isn't as good, not even half as good."
And he crumpled his painting
and threw it away.

"It must be the paints I have used today,"
Jason whispered, much too loud.
"I'll choose some others—

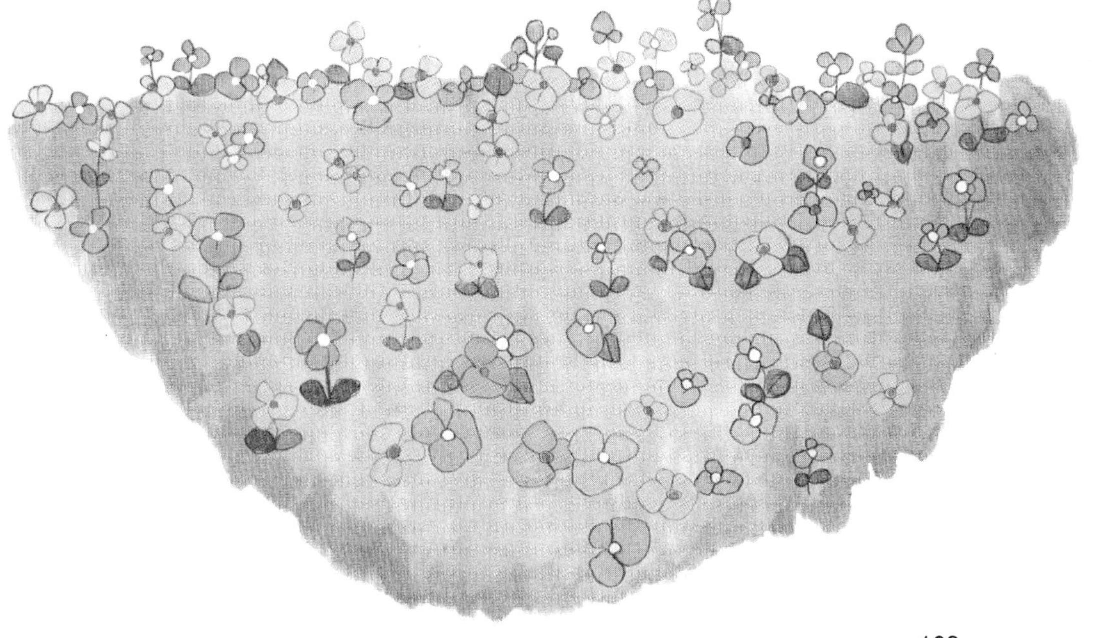

then I will paint a flower
that's better than any living flower.
That's what I will paint in the fields
tomorrow."

Jason took out his paints and easel.
He waved his brushes in the air.
The masterpiece began!

He painted the way
he thought he should paint
but the flowers in the field looked away.

Jason's flower that was to be better
than a field flower
wasn't better at all.
It had the reds and yellows and greens.
It had the blues and purples and browns.
But it didn't look like
any flower in the field.
It didn't look the best of all.

It wasn't even nearly as good!

So Jason crumpled up his painting
that day.

He crumpled it up and threw it away.
"It must be the flower that looked away,"
Jason whispered, much too loud.

"I'll choose another,
then I will paint a flower
that's better than any living flower.
That's what I will paint in the fields
tomorrow."

Jason took out his paints and easel.
He waved his brushes in the air.
The masterpiece began!

He painted strokes that were small and
some that were large
some were green and others blue,
Some were red,
there were yellow ones, too.
He painted the way
he thought he should paint,
but the flowers in the field looked away.

Jason frowned a very dark frown.
He looked at his painting,
then looked away.
It wasn't better than any flower
in the field.

It wasn't one bit as good.

Then Jason looked
at the flowers in the field.
They looked even more beautiful
than he had ever seen them.
They looked more beautiful
than his painted flowers,
the flowers he had thrown away.

Jason picked up his picture frame,
The frame that would frame
his masterpiece.
He held it up to one special flower
in the field,
The flower that had bowed away.

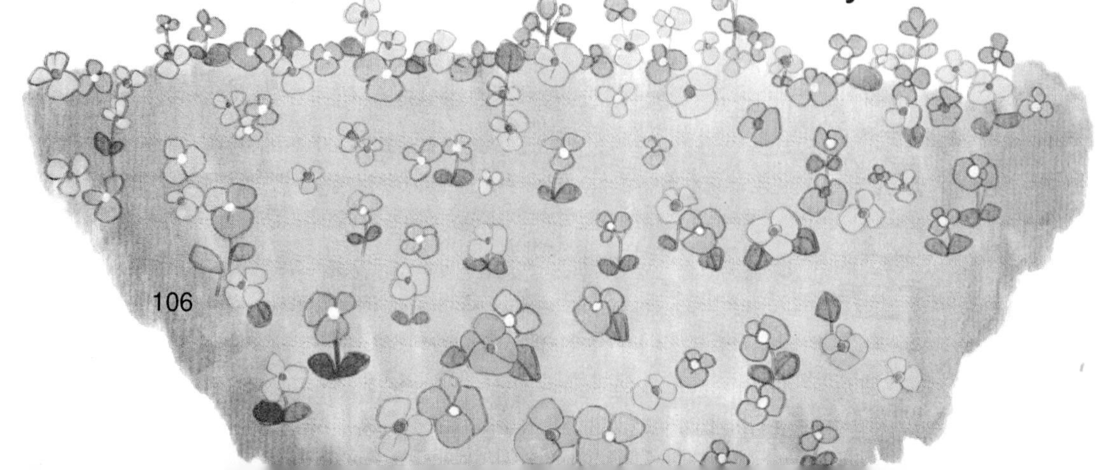

Trash

"The Painter who painted
this flower in my frame
is a better artist than I," he said.
"This flower is much better
than all those flowers
I crumpled and threw away.
This is a masterpiece!"

Butterflies and Brown Cocoons

If butterflies come from brown cocoons,
And flowers from little seeds,
Shouldn't I know that God supplies
Every one of tomorrow's needs?

Why Is a Bee Called a Bee?

Why is a bee called a bee?
Why isn't it called a cee?
You can't be a bee,
  but you could see a cee,
so why don't we call it a cee?

MOM

Why is a bee called a bee?
Why isn't it called a dee?
Then we'd have bumble dees
  and honey dees.
How confusing to call a bee dee!

Why is a bee called a bee?
Why isn't it called an eee?
If a bee goes B-uzz
  would an eee go E-uzz?
Is that why it's not called an eee?

Why is a bee called a bee?
Why isn't it called a pea?
If bees were called peas,
  would peas be called bees?
Then Mother would say, "Eat your bees."

Why is a bee called a bee?
Why isn't it called a zee?
Would the honey we eat
  just put us to sleep
if it came from honey bee zzzs?

So why is a bee called a bee?
Would you rather it be cee, dee, or eee?
If you really don't mind, I think you will
    find
that it's better to let the bee be!

Why Doesn't This Thing Work?

When spring comes we think of our gardens and lawns. Do people at your house do that? They do at the house where Kenny and Kathy live.

ON

One day Kenny took the garden hose from the garage. He tightened one end onto the faucet on the side of the house. Then Kenny picked up the other end of the garden hose. He pointed it at the flower bed and waited. But nothing came out.

"Why doesn't this thing work?" Kenny asked. He looked at the end of the hose. There was nothing in it to keep the water from coming out.

"We have to turn it on!" Kathy laughed. Kenny was still looking down into the end of the hose when Kathy turned the water on. What surprise do you think Kenny got?

Then Kathy and Kenny took the lawnmower from the garage. Kenny pulled on the starter rope. The lawnmower groaned and grunted. But it wouldn't start. Kenny pulled and pulled until he was too tired to pull anymore. But the lawnmower still would not start.

"Why doesn't this thing work?" Kenny wondered.

"Maybe we need a new lawnmower," said Kathy.

"Maybe we need gas in the tank," said Kenny. "I forgot to put gas in it." After Kenny filled it with gas he pulled the starter rope again. The lawnmower grunted once or twice. Then it started. Kenny mowed the lawn. That's what lawnmowers are for, aren't they?

Kathy took the electric grass clippers from the garage. She wanted to trim the grass along the sidewalk. Kathy carried the clippers to the sidewalk. She clicked the starter switch. But nothing happened. The clippers didn't move. They didn't even wiggle.

"Maybe we need new clippers," said Kenny.

"Maybe we need to plug the cord into the electric outlet," said Kathy. "I forgot to do that. Electric clippers won't clip if they are not plugged in, will they?"

Kathy plugged the end of the cord into the outlet. Then she clicked the starter switch. They worked! So Kathy neatly clipped the grass along the sidewalk.

That night at dinner Kathy and Kenny laughed about the things that didn't work.

They told Mother and Father about the hose that wouldn't give them water. They talked about the lawnmower that wouldn't mow. And they talked about the clippers that wouldn't clip.

"Many people are like that," said Father. "They want God to help them do things. But they don't even talk with him about these things. They don't remember to pray."

"Is prayer something like turning on the water, or filling a tank with gas, or plugging in an electric cord?" asked Kathy.

"If we want God's help, we have to turn it on or fill it up or plug it in," said Father. "That's what happens when we pray. Prayer makes lots of things work for us."

"I never thought of prayer that way," said Kenny.

"Neither have I," said Kathy.

Have you?

What Katy Did and Katy Didn't

Have you ever done what Katy did?
When Mother said "wash," Katy wouldn't.
"Please clean your room," but Katy didn't.
"Please make your bed," but Katy did not.

"Please help with the dishes,"
  but Katy said "No!"
"Please come with me,"
  but Katy wouldn't go.
I know you'd never do what Katy did.
You'd never say "no" or refuse to go
  when Mother asks or says you should.
I know you'd never do that.

Or would you?

You wouldn't do what Katy did.
You'd rather do what Katy didn't.

Or would you?

And you wouldn't say what Katy said.
When Mother said "eat," Katy said "won't."
"It's time to sleep," but Katy said "can't."
"Let's do our chores," but Katy said "no."
"Let's hang up your clothes,"
  but Katy said "not."

You'd never say "NO"
  when Mother says "YES."

Especially since Mother knows
that yes is best.

Or would you?

Have you ever gone where Katy went?
She went outside, away from Mother.
She went for a walk all alone.
She wanted to leave her chores that day
So she went to the park
at the edge of town.

And this is what Katy said that day,
"Mother won't tell me what to do,
I'll go where I want and play when I wish.
I won't wash even one more dish.
I'll eat all I want and sleep when I want.
I won't sweep the floor or make my old
bed.
Out here I can do what *I* want instead."

You wouldn't go where Katy went
and you wouldn't say what Katy said.
I know you wouldn't.

Or would you?

Have you ever found what Katy found?
When lunchtime came
  she found she was hungry.
Away from Mother, she found there were:
No dishes to wash, but no food either.
No bed to make, but no place to nap.
No room to clean, but no place to play.
No chores out here, but no home either.
No mother to obey, but no one to cuddle.

Perhaps you've found what Katy found—
that home seems better far away.
Perhaps you've found that too.

Have you?

Have you met a friend like Katy's friend?
She's tiny and soft with long pink ears.
She's on her own.
She has no room to sweep or clean.
No bed that's soft to snuggle in.
No one to help her do her chores
  or get her food or iron her clothes
  or wash her dishes or sew her buttons.
She has no mother to love or care for her.

Perhaps you've learned what Katy
learned—
Mother does more than you think she
does.
And Mother cares
more than you ever knew.
I'm sure you've already learned
these things,

haven't you?

Have you ever thought what Katy
thought?
Have you thought of a friend
like Katy's friend
who wished she had what Katy had?
Have you ever thought of all you have?
Have you ever thought about
what Mother does?
Have you thought about her loving care?
If you thought what Katy thought that day,
you'd do what Katy did.

Have you ever done what Katy did?
She ran back home as fast as she could.

She hugged her mother and kissed her
too.
She told her mother what she had
learned.
And she said she was sorry
for what she had done.

Perhaps you've done what Katy did.
Perhaps you've learned
what Mother does for you,
and told her how special she is.

You have done that,

haven't you?

There's one more thing that Katy did.
I know you'll want to do this too.
This is what Katy said,
"Happy Mother's Day, Mom,
on this special day! I love you."

You've done this too,

haven't you?

A Letter to My Grandma

Dear Grandma,
The other day a friend asked me,
"What's a grandma like?"

I guess you know by
now,
That my friend didn't
have one,
Or she wouldn't ask
such things.
I tried to tell her a
little
About what a
grandma is like.
But it's hard to tell
Something special
like that in
words.

This is what I told
her . . .
A grandma is a lot
like a mom,
Except her lap is a
little softer
And maybe there's a
little more of it.

She always has a cookie for me
In her cookie jar,
And a quarter for me
In her purse.

Grandma likes to sing to me
And read to me,
Almost as much as she
Likes to play with me.

When I have breakfast
At Grandma's house,
She always asks me,
"What would you like to eat?"
And that's what we eat!

Grandma likes to shop with me
And I like to shop with her
Because she almost always
Buys me something I want.

My mother says
  Grandma spoils me.
But I think
  she just loves me.

When I go to bed at night,
I know that Grandma prays for me.

I'm glad you're my grandma.
There's no one quite like you
In all the world.
Thanks, Grandma, for being my grandma.

I know it's Mother's Day,
But I also want to say,
"Happy Grandmother's Day!
I love you."

Me.

Planting Seeds

This week Mother and I planted seeds. I had thought there was only one way to plant seeds. But I found that there are many kinds of seeds and many ways to plant them.

On Monday we took rakes, hoes, packets of seeds, and fertilizer to the garden. We dug up the dirt and raked it until it was soft. It was fun to put the little seeds into the furrows we dug. We mixed fertilizer into the dirt and covered the seeds with the soft dirt.

Mother said clouds will drop rain on our seeds. And the sun will shine on the dirt and keep it warm. Soon little green sprouts will peek out of the ground. They will grow into tall, strong plants.

Bean plants will grow from the bean seeds. Radishes will grow from the radish seeds. Beets will grow from those strange little beet seeds. That's the way God planned for new plants to grow.

You should have seen Mother and me when we finished. We had sweat running down our faces. And we had lots of dirt on our hands.

On Tuesday, my sister went for a walk with us to a beautiful meadow. It had lots of dandelions everywhere. Some had yellow flowers but some were like little white, fluffy balls.

Sis picked a fluffy white dandelion ball. She blew on it. Hundreds of little seeds came out and sailed away on the wind. Sis thought this was fun. She picked another

fluffy white dandelion and blew on it. More little seeds came out. They sailed away on the wind also. Sis blew on many dandelion seed balls. You should have seen her!

Mother said that Sis was planting seeds, too. She was planting dandelion seeds. But Sis did not have to dig up dirt. She did not have to make furrows. She did not have to get dirty or mix in some fertilizer. God planned for dandelion seeds to be carried by the wind. He helps them plant themselves when they fall to the ground.

On Wednesday Mother read a Bible story to me. She told me how God does special things in the lives of his people. And she told me how God can do special things in my life, too.

Mother said she is planting seeds whenever she reads the Bible to me or my sister. She said God will help good things to grow in us because we have heard God's truth from his Word. She said that's the way God planned for his truth to grow in people.

Mother doesn't have to dig up dirt to plant God's truth seeds in me. All she has to do is read something from the Bible or pray with me. God helps his truth seeds to grow beautiful things in me. He also helps his truth seeds grow good things in you.

Aren't you glad that God planned for some seeds to fly with the wind and garden seeds to grow to give us good food? And aren't you glad he planned for his truth seeds to grow in us, too?

June

Number One

Mother knew that Joey was sad when he came home from school. Mothers always seem to know those kinds of things.

"Bad day at school?" she asked.

"We played softball today at school," said Joey, softly. "I was chosen *last* for our team. I didn't hit the ball once. And I made two really bad errors. I guess I'm just not very good."

"Very good what?" asked Mother.

"Very good anything," said Joey.

"You may not be as good as some others when you're playing softball," said Mother. "But Father and I think you're in first place. When I ask you to clean your room, you're number one. When your sister needs a friend, you're number one. You're number one in many ways."

Mother smiled one of her I've-got-a-good-idea smiles. She took a large blue button, some blue ribbon, a little piece of red ribbon and a yellow "1." Soon she had a special award for Joey. She pinned it on him. "When Father comes home, he'll see that you're in first place," she said.

What do you think Joey did when he heard Father open the door?

Mary's mother knew that she wasn't on top of the world when she came home from school.

"Tell me about it," said Mother.

"Tell you about what?" asked Mary.

"About the not-so-good things that happened today at school," said Mother.

Mary knew that Mother knew more than Mary thought she knew. Mothers are like that, aren't they?

"My friends were not good friends today," said Mary. "Judy made fun of my dress. Sally laughed at me for getting a bad grade on my paper. And Terry said I'm a loser because she got the part I wanted in the school play."

"I'm sorry that my number-one-daughter wasn't number one with her friends today," said Mother. "But you're still number one with Father and me. When it's time to set the table, you're a number-one-helper. When kitty needs someone to take care of her, you're a number-one-friend. And when it's time for you to pray, you have a number-one-heart. Father and I think you are number one in many ways."

Mother hugged Mary tightly. Then she said, "I'm going to give you a special gift so you can look at it when you're feeling sad."

Mary's eyes sparkled when Mother handed her a pretty vase with a big "1st" on it.

"When Father comes home, you can show him you're in first place!" said Mother.

What do you think Mary did when she heard Father open the door?

Flavors Are Fun

Tommy and Tanya stopped at the new ice cream shop. "What flavor of ice cream would you like?" the man asked, pointing at the long list on the wall.

Tanya looked at the list. She expected to

see three flavors—chocolate, vanilla, and strawberry. But there were more than thirty flavors.

"Where did all those flavors come from?" Tanya asked. "I never knew there were so many."

"Some came from berries, some from fruit, and some from nuts," said the man. "Some came from nearby places and others came from far away. Some came from things that are red or orange or yellow or blue or purple or brown."

"Wow! Could we guess which ones are which?" asked Tommy.

"Okay, let's have a little game," said the man. "I have five plastic spoons for each of you. Close your eyes and tell me what flavor you taste."

The man gave each one a small spoonful of one ice cream. "Guess the flavor, the color, and where the flavor came from," said the man.

"Banana," said Tommy. "It's yellow."

"And it comes from far away," added Tanya.

"Good," said the man. "See how easy this game is?"

Then the man gave each another small spoonful of ice cream. "Guess this one," he said.

"Some kind of mint," said Tanya. "But it also tastes a little like chocolate. Is it brown?"

"You got part of it right," said the man. "It's mint chocolate. But it's green. Chocolate, which can be either brown or white when we eat it, comes from the beans or seeds of the cacao tree. It grows in places like Brazil or Nigeria. But we grow lots of mint right around here."

Strawberry was easy to guess. They both guessed red and that it grew nearby. Blueberry was easy too. Blueberries grew not too far away. But the color was tricky. Tommy and Tanya said blue. The berries in the ice cream were blue. But the ice cream was a creamy yellow or white.

"Okay, here's one that won't be as easy as you think," said the man.

"Vanilla," Tanya and Tommy said together. But Tanya thought vanilla ice cream was yellow and Tommy thought it was white. The man said they were both right.

"But where do we get vanilla?" he asked. Of course, neither of them knew. Do you?

"This will surprise you," said the man. "Vanilla comes from beans. But these beans grow on a type of orchid vine."

"Does that mean it is lavender color?" asked Tanya.

"Not really," said the man. "The beans are chocolate color. But vanilla ice cream is a creamy color, a whitish yellow, with tiny specks of the bean all through it."

"All that from plain old vanilla!" said Tommy. "But where does the flavor come from?"

"Plain old vanilla really isn't plain," said the man. "When you get real vanilla, it's a very special flavor. We get it from places like Mexico, Madagascar, and Tahiti. Orchid beans from these faraway places give us a good flavor."

"I'll always think more of vanilla from now on," said Tanya.

Before long Tommy and Tanya and the ice cream man had talked about peach and

apple trees, walnut and pecan trees, berry plants and grape vines. They also talked about pineapples and macadamia nuts from Hawaii and coconuts from faraway coconut palms.

By this time the man gave Tommy and Tanya the ice cream that they ordered. It really tasted good.

"I know something else that is special about flavors," said Tommy.

"What's that?" asked the ice cream man.

"God gave us the gift of taste so that we can know each flavor when we eat it," said Tommy.

"And since God made each tree or bush or vine or plant, he really makes each flavor," said Tanya.

"Then we should thank him for our ice cream," said Tommy. So they did.

Do you have a favorite flavor? You will remember to thank God the next time you taste a good flavor, won't you? And remember to thank him for the gift of taste that he gave you.

It's Much More Fun with You

I want to go canoeing
In my little birch canoe.
But canoeing is no fun alone;
It's much more fun with you.

I want to have a picnic
  With a picnic lunch for two.
But a picnic is no fun to eat,
  Unless I eat with you.

I want to hike outside tonight
  And hear an owl go "whoo."
But hiking can be quite scary
  Unless I'm there with you.

I like to hear a story
  Of a tale that's old or new.
But what's the fun of hearing one
  Unless it's shared with you?

I like to pray at bedtime
  I know that you do, too.
So remember when *you* pray tonight
  That *I* will pray for you.

When I Become a Man

"What will you do when you grow up?"
his aunt asked Danny today.
"What will you do and what will you be?

It's time to think and it's time to plan.
It's time to think about becoming a man.

Danny thought about what his aunt said.
He thought as he went for a walk
through town.
"What will I do? How do I know?
But it's time to think and it's time to plan.
I really must know before I become a
man."

When Danny came to Fourth and Main,
he saw a policeman standing there.
He looked tall and straight with his uni-
form.
So Danny thought about a possible plan.
"Perhaps I can be a policeman
when I become a man."

Then a fire engine roared out
the firehouse door.
Sirens whined and firemen waved.
They looked so brave as they rode along.
So Danny thought about
another possible plan.
"Perhaps I can be a fireman
when I become a man."

Danny thought he liked that plan
until a pilot hurried by.
He was going to the airport
where he would fly.
Perhaps he would fly a big plane around
the world.
So Danny thought again
about a possible plan.

"Perhaps I can be a pilot
when I become a man."

But there were more. There were many more.
Danny saw them all as he stood by a store.
There were lawyers and doctors
and milkmen, too.
Each time Danny wondered
what he should do.
Each time he thought about a possible plan.
"Perhaps I can be that
when I become a man.

"Should I be a soldier or sailor then?
Should I work in an office or run a bank?
Should I make tall buildings?
What should I do?"
Each time he thought about a possible plan
and thought he could do that
when he became a man.

Danny was still thinking hard
when he came back home.

He thought of policemen and firemen, too.
He thought of all the men
he had seen that day.
And he thought of each possible plan
and wondered what he would be
when he became a man.

Then Danny saw his father sitting there.
He was sitting with his Bible
in his favorite chair.
He knew what a great dad
his dad had been.
Then Danny thought of
a super great plan.
"I want to be just like
Dad
when I become a
man!"

A Letter to My Grandpa

Dear Grandpa,
The other day a friend asked me,
"What's a grandpa like?"

I guess you
know by
now,
That he didn't
have one,
Or he wouldn't
ask such
things.

I tried to tell him a
little
About what a
grandpa is like.
But it's hard to tell
Something special
like that in words.
This is what I told
him . . .

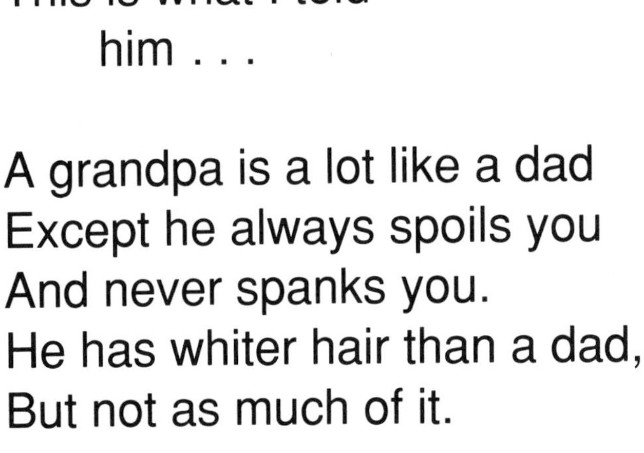

A grandpa is a lot like a dad
Except he always spoils you
And never spanks you.
He has whiter hair than a dad,
But not as much of it.

A grandpa smiles like sunshine
And showers gifts like rain.
When I come to my grandpa's house,
I meet his arms first,
Then the rest of him.
He gives big hugs
And little pieces of candy.
He always has time to play,
Even when I know he doesn't.

A grandpa asks me questions
About me.
He wants to know
What other people don't even care about,
And what makes me such a good boy.

A grandpa likes to say yes
And hates to say no.
When I'm with Grandpa,
I'm the most important person
In the world.
A king or prince
Would not get more
    of Grandpa's attention
Than I do.

When I go
to bed at night,
I know that
Grandpa
prays for me.

I'm glad you're my grandpa.
There's no one quite like you
In all the world.

Thanks, Grandpa, for being my grandpa.

I know it's Father's Day,
But I also want to say,
"Happy Grandfather's Day.

I love you."

Me.

July

This Warm Summer Day

"Where have you been
  on this warm summer day?"

"I went to find a gift for you."

"What did you find
  on this warm summer day?"

“I found a gift that says,
‘I LOVE YOU.’”

A Balloon for Every Blessing

Jennifer grumbled and Jennifer complained. "Why do ALL my friends have better clothes?" she asked. "Why do they ALL have better houses? Why do they ALL have better everything?"

"ALL?" Mother asked. "Do ALL your friends have more than you?"

"Yes, every one of them," Jennifer grumbled. "I don't have anything!"

"Not anything?" Mother asked. "I didn't know we had so little. Why don't we go for a walk in the park? We can talk about it there."

Jennifer grumbled all the way to the park. She complained as they walked through the park.

"Now what is it that we don't have?" Mother asked.

Jennifer thought for a minute. Maybe two. "Mary has a 40-inch TV and ours is only a 19-inch one," Jennifer grumbled. "Priscilla has her own TV in her room, and I don't."

Mother smiled. She almost laughed. But she didn't. (Would you?)

"I didn't realize we were so poor," Mother said. Jennifer looked at Mother. She didn't think Mother sounded sincere about that.

"What else don't we have?" Mother asked.

"Well, Susan has a beautiful horse, and

all I have is a dog and a cat," Jennifer complained.

"Poor girl," said Mother.

Jennifer didn't like the way Mother said that. She didn't sound sincere.

"Anything else?" Mother asked.

"Clara has a pool in her back yard, and we don't," said Jennifer.

"Really?" said Mother. "I feel sorry for us."

Jennifer was sure that Mother was not sincere about that. "You don't mean that, do you?" she asked.

"No, I don't," said Mother. "Think of all you DO have. Those are your blessings. You have so many of them."

"Do I have as many blessings as that man has balloons?" asked Jennifer.

Mother looked at the balloon man coming toward them. He had lots of big balloons.

"More!" said Mother. Then Mother had an idea.

"What blessings do you have?" Mother asked. "Tell me. I'll buy you a balloon for each one."

Jennifer thought this would be fun.

(Wouldn't you?) So she began to tell Mother about each of her blessings.

"I have a wonderful dad," she said.

"Here's one balloon," said Mother. "Don't you think a wonderful dad is better than a 40-inch TV?"

Jennifer smiled. "And a wonderful mom," she added.

"Is that better than a horse?" Mother asked as she gave the second balloon to Jennifer. Jennifer laughed. She wouldn't trade her mother for a thousand horses.

Jennifer talked about her Sunday school and church, her good friends, her brother, and her beautiful room. She even decided that her house was quite special after all (even without a swimming pool).

Soon the balloon man had nothing left in his hands. Jennifer was holding all his balloons.

Jennifer kept on telling her blessings.

"I have no more balloons," said the balloon man.

"I have lots more blessings," said Jennifer. "I guess I have more blessings than balloons."

Do you?

The Best Parade Ever

It's no fun when your very best friend breaks his leg. Eric knew that it was no fun for Bobby to stay inside all day. And it was no fun for Eric either. He felt sorry because his friend was hurting.

Eric wondered what he could do to cheer his friend. What would you do if you were Eric? Eric knew that it had to be something special because Bobby was special. But what?

"Why don't I send a parade past his house?" Eric thought. "But it must be a big parade. It must be the very best parade ever."

Eric could see the parade in his mind. It would have elephants and zebras,

lions and giraffes, calliopes and organ grinders. And, of course, every parade must have lots of people playing music.

There would be horn-tooters and drum-beaters, whistle-blowers and baton twirlers. Nothing less than a dozen of each would do. Maybe two dozen of each would be better.

Before long, Eric's daydream parade was a mile long. Eric thought it might even become two miles long. But there was nothing too good for his friend with the broken leg.

Eric's parade was the most wonderful

parade ever. He had never seen a better parade than the one he saw in his mind.

Eric was so happy about his special parade. He jumped up and started to run. He would get his parade together now!

But suddenly Eric stopped. Where would he find all those things? Where would he get all the animals and musicians? Where would he find the calliopes and organ grinders?

Suddenly Eric felt sad. He knew that there wasn't one calliope in his town. There wasn't one organ grinder either. There wasn't one elephant or zebra or giraffe. There wasn't one thing that he needed for his parade.

Then Eric remembered something. There *was* one thing for the parade. Eric ran home as fast as he could. Before long, he was back at his friend's house.

Eric marched in front of Bobby's window. He beat on his drum. "Boom, BOOM, boom!" went Eric's drum. Bobby looked out the window. He smiled. There was his own special parade, with his own special friend.

There were no elephants or lions or zebras or giraffes. There were no horn-tooters or baton twirlers. There were no calliopes or organ grinders. But there was one VERY SPECIAL drum beater.

Don't you think Bobby was happy that day? He had the best parade ever because Eric was his very best friend, and Eric's parade was just for him. That really is quite special, isn't it?

A Family Is Fun

A family is fun, I think you'll agree,
whether the family is one, two, or three.
It really doesn't matter how many there
are,
until you squeeze into the old family car.

There's a puppy,
a hamster,
a goldfish or two,
a pigeon,
canary,
and stuffed kangaroo.

For a family is never a family yet
until it collects every imaginable pet.

A family is fun, I think you should know,
whether we're swimming or out in the
snow.
We may be making a snowman or two
or cutting up paper or gluing with glue.
We'll go to the circus or stop at the store.
And whatever we do, we'll always do
more.
We'll go to the park or visit the zoo.
We'll go on a picnic. Can you go, too?

A family is fun, a super success,
except when Sarah spilled ink on her
dress.
And kitty fell into the bowl with our fish,
when puppy chased her away from his
dish.
Then Randy and Sandy got into a fight,
'cause each thought the other
just couldn't be right.

A family is fun, as anyone knows
who has trimmed and scrubbed
sixty-three dirty toes.

Sixty-three?
Could it be?
We miscounted tonight?
I know sixty-three just couldn't be right!
I'd better go back
and count them once more.
Who knows—I may find
that there are sixty-four!

A family is fun, a family is fine
until you must stand in the family bath
line.
It's really no fun when Sis beats me there
and spends half the morning
to blow dry her hair.

A family is fun, we dine like kings,
on hamburgers,
hot dogs,
milkshakes,
and things.
We get scratches
and cuts,
poison ivy
and sneezes.

We share every sniffle
  and many diseases.

But a family is fun, that really is true.
We never run out of fun things to do.
Where else can you laugh
  and do things together,
in all kinds of places
  and all kinds of weather?
Where else can you have
  such wonderful friends?
It's one friendship
  that never, ever ends!

Yes, our family is great,
  I'm glad for each one in it
And I'm thankful that God
  is with us each minute.

Tippy

August

Ups and Downs

The other day I heard Mother and Father talking. This is what I heard Mother say, "Life certainly has its ups and downs."

Later, when Mother was alone, I asked her what she meant. She told me about a friend of hers. When she was married she was so happy. Things really were up for her. Then her husband left her. They got divorced. Life went DOWN then. Mother said it really went way down.

Later Father told me about a man at his office. He was doing well in his work. He was even promoted several times. Things were up for him. Then he did something he shouldn't. Father said his boss had to fire the man. Things went down very fast for him. His family thought things really went down in a hurry for all of them.

I asked Mother if she and Father ever had ups and downs. She laughed.

"Lots of them," she said. She told me about some of the ups, the good times she and Father had. Each up was special. There really were a lot of them. Then she told about some of the downs. When they got married they didn't have much money. Both of them had to work very hard. It wasn't easy. That was a down. She told me about the times we got sick and the times we had to move. Those were downs, too.

Mother said that she and Father don't always agree, though they don't argue and fight like some parents. They really want to do things together. When they don't, that's down.

"It must be a down for you when I don't obey," I told Mother. She smiled. I knew that meant yes.

I told Mother that kids also have ups and downs. She smiled and said, "I know. I was a little girl one time." I had forgotten that.

Then Mother asked about my ups and downs. I told her that things really look up when she and Father are happy. Things look up when we do fun things together as a family.

"What about downs?" Mother asked.

I told Mother that it's really a down when a friend seems unfriendly or pretends that she's not my friend. Things are down when kids at school make fun of me or are mean to me. Things are down when someone laughs at me because I don't do something well.

"It's a very bad down when we try to put ourselves up by putting others down," said Mother. "I hope you never try to look good by making someone else look bad."

I hope I don't either! I'll have to think about that.

"Not all downs come from other people," said Mother. "We often take ourselves down when we do down things."

"Like what?" I asked.

"Like not telling the truth," said Mother. "That usually gets us into trouble, and trouble is a down. If we're mean to someone else that makes us feel mean about ourselves. That's a down. And when we do something we know is wrong. That's *really* a down."

"What's a special up for you?" I asked Mother.

"To know that you and Father truly love me," said Mother. "We can feel up even when we have a lot of downs if we know that someone important loves us very much."

"Is that why we feel up when we know that Jesus loves us?" I asked.

"Yes," said Mother.

"That's the best up of all! When we keep looking up to Jesus, he helps us through our downs. And he helps us have more ups."

I guess I want Jesus to help me up, even when I feel down. And I want him to help me help others up when they feel down. Would you like that, too?

What's on the Other Side?

Yesterday I looked into a hollow log. There was a big wide world on the other side. It looked like the world I live in. The bunny on the other side looked just like a bunny I saw near the log.

Do you suppose that place on the other

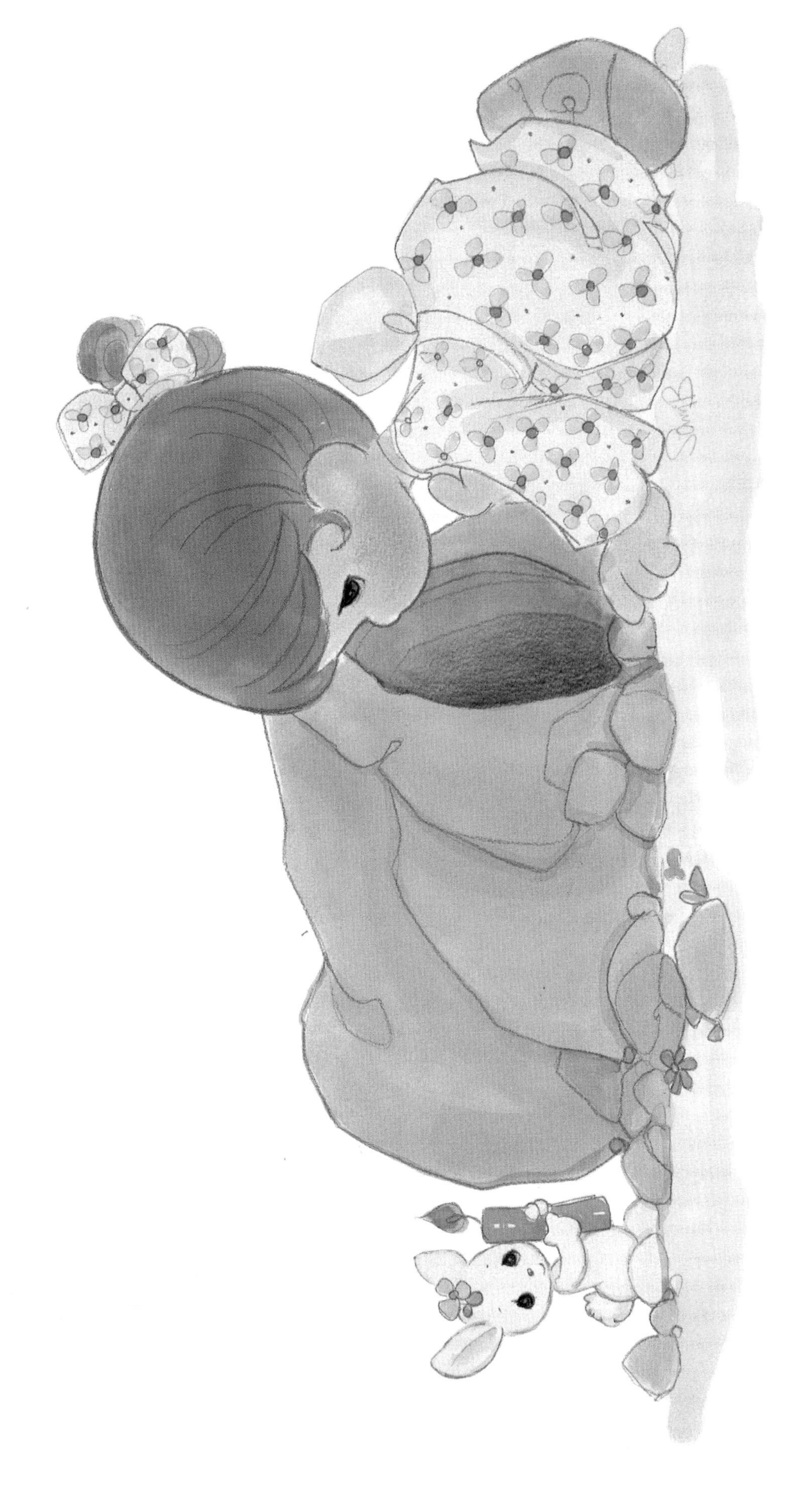

side of the hollow log is just like the place where I am? Maybe it is. If I'm happy here, I would probably be happy there. If I'm unhappy here, I would probably be unhappy there. If I grumble here, I would probably grumble there, too.

This morning I looked at the mirror in my room. There was someone on the other side of the mirror. And there was a room on the other side, too.

When I smiled, the girl in the mirror smiled back at me. When I moved back, she moved back, too. Mother said the girl on the other side of the mirror looks just like me. She must be my twin, or something like that. I guess she's a special person.

The room on the other side of the mirror looks just like my room. Do you suppose this special someone lives just the way I do in a room just like mine? I wonder what it would be like to live on the other side of my mirror. Mother said she thought it would be just like living here. If I like to have good friends here, I would probably like to have good friends there. If I don't obey here, I probably would not obey there.

This afternoon Mother wanted me to do some chores. I wanted to play. I grumbled and complained. I said something like, "I wish I didn't live here any more. Then I wouldn't have to do my old chores any more."

Mother smiled. "Would you rather live on the other side of the log?" she asked. "Or would you rather live on the other side of your mirror? You'd probably have the same chores there. And Mother there would also want you to do them."

Do you know what? I think Mother is right. And I think I would really rather stay on this side of the log. I'd rather stay on this side of my mirror, too. Wouldn't you?

Do You Ever Make Mistakes?

Do you ever make mistakes? I do. Some of them are little mistakes. Some of them are not so little.

But what do you do when you make a mistake? I'll tell you what I do. Sometimes I say that my brother did it. That's not very nice, is it? At other times I say that kitty or puppy must have done it.

And sometimes I have to say that I did it. But it wasn't my fault. That crazy car just hit the meter all by itself. Do you think anyone believes me when I say that? No, I guess not.

Sometimes I get angry when I make a mistake. Sometimes I cry. Sometimes I even scream. But none of these things really helps.

Do you know what I've found helps the most? When I make a mistake now, I try to pray. God knows I'm not perfect. He knows I may make another mistake tomorrow. But he forgives me. I'll forgive you when you make your next mistake.

I know my mistake made you very unhappy. I'm really VERY, VERY sorry. I hope you'll forgive me now. So thank you for forgiving me. You will, won't you?

Here Can Be Better Than There

George Gimme Getaway Gare
  wants to go somewhere,
  but doesn't know where.
He wants to go anywhere
    as long as it's not here,
and that, I suppose,
    must be somewhere out there.

George wants to be someone he's not,
and he's really quite tired
of all he's now got.

George is bored with everything Here,
and that is why he wants to be There.
Yes, There is the place
George wants to go,
though what is There he doesn't know.

George doesn't care about what is There
as long as he gets away from Here.
What's wrong with Here?
It's what he's now got.
And he's more concerned
with what he has not.

George is packed and ready for There,
though he's found that There
can be anywhere.
It can be any place that isn't Here.
So how can he go just anywhere?
How will he know
when he's really There?

THIS WAY
NO THIS WAY

Now you see the problem
that George has got.
It's the problem of wanting
to go where he's not.
It's the problem of trying
to leave what he's got.
It's the problem of trying
to be someone he's not.

George Gimme Getaway Gare
lives down your street,
almost anywhere.
He's a kid on your block
or a kid next door,
almost any kid
who thinks he wants more.

George is a kid like us kids everywhere.
We have everything Here
but wish we were There.

I hope you will talk with
George G. G. Gare
before he leaves Here
and tries to go There.

When George gets There,
He will wish he were Here,
For Here looks the best
    when you finally get There.

Do you ever wish
    you were somewhere you're not,
    or someone you're not?

Ask G. G. G. Gare what you've got.
You've got a lot!

Don't wish what you haven't
    instead of what you've got,
for something out There
    that maybe is not.
For if you were There
    with what is not,
you'd wish you were Here
    with all you've now got.

Are you thankful, quite thankful,
    for what you've now got?
Would you like to thank Someone
    right Here on the spot?

September

There's a Worm in My Apple

Summer was over for Eddie McGee.
It was back to school on September 3.
It was back to school on a sunny day—
when he'd rather, much rather,
stay home to play.
He tried to think of some kind of rule
that would help him stay home
and not go to school.

Ed had an excuse, in fact he had four.
But Mother had heard each one before.
So Ed McGee started again
to engineer a better plan.
But you'd have to be smart,
you really would,
to outsmart Mom,
who knows what's good.

You know how Ed feels,
I know that you do.
When school days begin,
you'd rather play, too.
You dread doing math and so you act sick.
You develop fake sneezes
with imaginary diseases.

But Mom knows your game
she certainly does.
Whatever you plan, it already was.
And every time you try a new scheme,
she knows that the scheme
is only a dream.
So you may as well plan
on school the first day.
That's what I think your mother will say.

Now teachers like apples,
that's what Mom said.
And she told Ed to take one
that's bright shiny red.
But Ed was still feeling
quite grumpy and snide,
so he chose a bad apple
with a worm inside.

But somewhere on his way to school
Ed remembered a verse called
The Golden Rule.
He thought what he'd want if he were she.
He wouldn't want worms from Eddie
McGee.
He'd not want an apple that's sure to of-
fend,
but one that would say,
"I'm your new friend."

So Ed junked the apple,
the one with the worm,
that would make his teacher
shriek and squirm.
And he got another one fit for a queen
and washed it
and wiped it
all squeaky clean.

Then Ed was glad
he remembered that Rule.
He was even glad now
to go back to school.

Because you COUNT
My Sewing Tools
SamB

OATS
BEANS
TEA
JAM

The Chalk Didn't Do It!

"It's that silly chalk's fault!" Scotty moaned. You can see what the chalk did, can't you?

Sometimes numbers cause problems. Sometimes words cause problems. And sometimes people cause problems.

This time Scotty thought his chalk caused the problem in school. Somehow Scotty knew that 2 x 2 did not equal 9. But that's what his chalk said when it wrote on the little blackboard.

Scotty was thinking about a lot of other things when he wrote that. He really wasn't thinking about 2 x 2. He should have been. But he wasn't. He was daydreaming. Somehow he thought the chalk should write the right number anyway.

Do you think it was the chalk that made the mistake? Or was it Scotty?

"You can do it," said the teacher. "Try again!"

Scotty tried again. Now look what that chalk did! Anyone knows that 2 x 2 does not equal 6. You know that, don't you? But Scotty's chalk didn't know it. So you can see what happened. You can see why Scotty said once more, "That chalk just won't do anything right."

Do you think it was his chalk that couldn't do it right? Or was it Scotty?

2+2 = 9
2+2 = 6
2+2 = 3
2+2 = 4

"Try once more," said the teacher. "I know you can do it."

"I *can* do it," said Scotty. "It's this chalk that doesn't do it right."

"I see," said the teacher. "Well, what if you told the chalk the right number to write. Perhaps it will do what you tell it to do."

Scotty tried again. That's closer, isn't it? But the chalk went too far this time, didn't it? Anyone knows that 2 x 2 does not equal 3. But Scotty didn't write that. Scotty was daydreaming again. He forgot to tell the chalk the right number.

"That's close," said the teacher. "You almost have it right now. Once more and I think you will do it. This time, be sure to let your chalk know what *you* know."

Scotty picked up his chalk. He looked at it. "Do it right!" he said. The chalk didn't say a thing. Scotty started to daydream again. But he stopped and looked at the chalk.

"It isn't the chalk," Scotty whispered to himself. "It's the kid holding the chalk. Scotty, YOU do it right." This time Scotty didn't daydream.

Now you see what happened. Scotty did what he knew he should do. So the chalk did what it should do. That's a good lesson for Scotty—and all of us—to learn, isn't it?

If You Love Me

If you love me—
Will you give me
Everything I ask
of you?

If I love you—
I will give you
Only what is best
For you.

If you love me—
You won't hurt me,
Not the smallest hurt
Will do.

If I love you—
I must hurt you
When the hurt
Is best for you.

An Un-bearable Ouchy

Have you never a care
like Timothy Bear,
who thought he was quite lucky?
Until one day
he was heard to say,
"I'm beginning to feel quite yukky."

When Tim reached the nurse
he was feeling much worse.
He was grumbly and gritchy and grouchy.
But the nurse put Tim Bear
up on her small chair,
and gave him one more ouchy.

"Don't you care?
Don't you see,
that your shot has hurt me?
It really made me yelp."
But the nurse said to Bear,
"Yes, I really do care,
and my shot is the way to help."

Sometimes folks give us shots
or other whatnots
and we wonder why they do.
But if these hurts help
we should not yelp,
because they say, "I love you."

Listen!

Randy liked to play his guitar and sing. But he wasn't very good. That's because he liked to play and sing more than he liked to practice. Do you know anyone like that?

"Will you listen to me play and sing?" Randy asked his friend Rick one day.

Rick listened for about two minutes. Then

suddenly he was gone. He mumbled some excuse about having to rake leaves. But he didn't need to say anything. Randy knew why he left.

Before long, another friend, Johnny, came along. "Will you listen to me play and sing?" Randy asked.

Johnny listened for about a minute. Then suddenly he was gone. He also mumbled some excuse about cleaning up the yard. But Randy knew why he left. Johnny didn't need an excuse.

"I guess no one wants to listen to me," said Randy. So he began to play and sing for himself. He played. He sang. He almost thought his music was better than it really was.

Suddenly Randy looked up. There was his dog, Lance, who was listening as though this was the finest music in the world. It wasn't, of course. But Randy was playing and singing. So Lance thought it was terrific.

Randy sang a dozen or so songs for Lance. Lance listened cheerfully to each one and wagged his tail to applaud.

"You're a great listener," said Randy. "You listen to me even when I'm not very good. I guess you listen to me because I'm me—someone you love."

Then Randy thought about what he had just said. "I guess that's why Mom and Dad listen to me whenever I talk with them," he said to himself. "It's not that I have something great to say. They listen because I'm the one talking. They care. They listen because they love me."

Then Randy thought more about that. "I guess that's why God listens to me whenever I talk with him," he said. "He doesn't listen because I have an important speech to make. He cares. He listens because he loves me. He really wants to hear what I say, because I'm saying it."

Then Randy began to play and sing again. As long as Randy played, Lance listened.

Do you think what Randy said is true? If it is, we should remember it, shouldn't we?

Flying High

Once there was a boy named Alan who liked to walk outside and think about God. Every time he saw a cloud he thought about the wonderful things that God had made. Alan often sat down on the green grass and looked up into the sky.

Sometimes he saw clouds shaped like animals. One big cloud looked like an elephant. A much smaller cloud was like a little lamb. There were many other cloud animals in the sky, too. Alan knew that God made each cloud. He wanted to find a way to get closer to God. If he could ride on one of those clouds, would that help him get closer to God?

At other times Alan climbed into a tree. He felt the rough bark and listened to the wind sighing among the leaves. In September he might see an acorn or an apple hanging from a branch while the leaves drifted down. Alan knew that God made all these things

grow. He wanted to find a way to get closer to God. If he could climb to the top of the highest tree in the world, would that help him get closer to God?

Alan liked to climb up on a high hill near his home. He looked at the houses and fences and fields below. He could see far away. He could see many things. He knew that God had made every living thing that he saw—all the plants and animals and people down below. The boy wanted to find a way to get closer to God. If he could climb up on the highest hill in the world, would that help him get closer to God?

Alan talked with his friends about these things—about the clouds, the trees, and the high hills. He told them how he wanted to find a way to get closer to God. He asked them which way they thought was best.

One friend said, "There is no God." Another friend said, "There is a God. But why bother to get closer to him? He probably doesn't care about us anyway." A third friend said he thought it was a good idea to get closer to God because God really does care about us. But he also said that clouds and trees and hills are not high enough. He said Alan should fly high into the sky. That would help him get closest to God.

So Alan sat down and began to think about flying. He pretended to make a special little plane. He even gave it a special name, "Heaven Bound." In his mind he pretended to fly this plane far above the clouds. He went higher and higher until he thought he must be flying near the front door of heaven. But Alan did not feel any closer to God up there than he did down below on the ground.

That night Alan talked with his father about all these things. He asked his father

why he did not seem closer to God in his little plane.

Alan's dad smiled. He told Alan that God is not "up there" somewhere. He is "down here" with us. God promised to be with us each day. And he told Alan that the best way to get closer to God is to read his Book, the Bible, and talk with him often.

So Alan did exactly what his father had said. He read God's Book, the Bible. And he prayed.

Then he really and truly felt closer to God than he ever had before.

October

Jonathan C.

Jonathan C.,
  a big boy is he.
A very big boy is
  Jonathan C.
He's as big a boy
  as a boy could be.
That's how big is
  Jonathan C.

CHAMP

Jonathan C.,
  a very big boy is he.
He's so big
  all the team wants
Jonathan C.
  That's how big is
Jonathan C.

Jonathan C.,
  how big is he?
He's so big
  all the guys are afraid,
you see.
  That's how big is
Jonathan C.

Jonathan C.,
  what a man is he!
He's a man as much
  as a man can be.
That's how big is
  Jonathan C.

Jonathan C.
is bigger than me
and I stretch up
to an elephant's knee.
That's how big is
Jonathan C.

Jonathan C.
wants to play
with me,
but I feel like a
flea
when he's
with me.
That's how
big is
Jonathan
C.

Jonathan C.
is as big as three.
"All the pro teams want me,"
says he.
That's how big is
Jonathan C.

Jonathan C.,
a giant is he.
No one's as big,
I think you'll agree.
That's how big is
Jonathan C.

Jonathan C.,
how big is he?
"How big is BIG?"
asks Jonathan C.
"That's how big is
Jonathan C."

So if you want to play
with Jonathan C.,
you'd better be big,
as big as he.
You may want to bring
your own referee,
'cause there's a big boy, that
Jonathan C.

But now it's bedtime for
Jonathan C.
It's time to sit on Mother's knee.
"Tell me a story about God,"
says he.
Now *there's* someone bigger than
Jonathan C.

Little Mouse Under the Pumpkin Leaf

Little Mouse under the pumpkin leaf,
where will you sleep tonight?
Where is your house, and what is it
like?

Is there a kitchen with table and chairs?
Do you have carpets,
perhaps an upstairs?
Is there a place for a welcome mat,
Welcoming all but the neighborhood
cat?
Do you have a front door
for friends that are new?
And a door in the back
for old friends, too?

Little Mouse under the pumpkin leaf,
where will you sleep tonight?
Where is your house and what is it like?
Is there a place I can
call and find what
is there on your table,
or what there is not?
Will you have some
tasty food there?
Do you have your own
special chair?
Will dinner be served at
your table tonight—

With napkins and spoons
and soft candlelight?

Little Mouse under the pumpkin leaf,
where will you sleep tonight?
Where is your house and what is it like?
Do you have a soft bed to
cuddle down in—
With covers to pull
all the way to your chin?
Will your mother read stories
and kiss you good-night?
Will you sleep by the light
of a soft night light?
Do you sleep in your own
room upstairs?
Do Mother and Dad have you say
your own prayers?

Little Mouse under the pumpkin leaf,
where will you sleep tonight?
Where is your house and what is it like?
Can anyone see your little house—
The house just right for a wee, tiny
mouse?

Should I worry that no one
will take care of you?
No, I won't worry. I know it is true,
That the Someone who sees
the things I do,
Watches over a Little Mouse, too.

Nails

thank you God for Everything
SPINACH

November

Thank You!

"Thank you for the wonderful turkey dinner," Michael said to his grandmother. It was always special to come to Grandmother's and Grandfather's farm for Thanksgiving Dinner.

"You are welcome," Grandmother said with a big smile. "But I'm not the only one who helped you have this wonderful turkey dinner."

Michael remembered that Mother had brought the vegetables. Aunt Ellen had brought the salad. Aunt Elizabeth had brought the dessert.

Michael thanked Aunt Ellen. He thanked Aunt Elizabeth. And he thanked Mother, too.

"I'm glad you are thankful," said Mother. "But there are others who helped us have this wonderful meal."

Michael thought about this. Then he remembered that Uncle Henry earned money to buy things for the dessert. Uncle Charles earned money to buy things for the salad. Father earned money to buy the vegetables. And Grandfather earned money to buy the turkey.

Michael thanked Uncle Henry. He thanked Uncle Charles. He thanked Grandfather. And he thanked Father.

"I'm glad you're thankful to us," said Fa-

ther. "You are a very thoughtful boy. But others helped us have this wonderful Thanksgiving Dinner. Do you know who?"

Michael tried to think of others. But he couldn't think of anyone else who had brought food or earned money to buy it.

"Let's start with the grocers who sold us all these things," said Father. "Grocers help us get good food from many different places."

"I'm thankful for the grocers," said Michael. "But where did the grocers get the food?"

Then Father and Michael thought about other people who helped them get their Thanksgiving Dinner. Michael thought about the farmers who raised the vegetables. He thought about the people who raised the turkey. He thought about the dairy farmer whose cows gave milk and cream for the ice cream.

"And how did all of these people get their food to the grocer?" asked Father.

Michael remembered the butchers who got the turkeys ready to sell. He thought of the people who drove the trucks and the engineers who ran the trains that hauled all the food. He thought of other people who handled it along the way.

Michael soon had a long list of people who helped them have a wonderful Thanksgiving Dinner. "I can't thank each of them in person," said Michael. "But I am thankful for each and every one."

"There's one more person you *can* thank,"

said Father. "He helped us have everything on the table and a lot more."

Michael thought for a long time. Then he remembered. "God gave us everything we ate," he said. "And I can thank him!"

Michael went outside where he could be alone. Do you know what he did out there?

I'm Thankful for Brushes and Brooms

I heard Mom say as she scrubbed today,
"I'm thankful for brushes and brooms.
I'm glad to clean my cozy house
That's filled with cheerful rooms."

I heard Mom say at the washing machine,
"I'm thankful for dirty clothes.
I'm glad that I have a healthy child
Who can play each day she grows."

I heard Mom say at the sink tonight,
"I'm thankful for dirty dishes.
I'm glad we filled our plates with food
Instead of empty wishes."

I heard Mom say in her prayers tonight,
"I'm thankful for problems today.
If life never got a little bit rough,
I might forget to pray."

Where Does Winter Come From?

Where does winter come from?
And where does summer go?
Who makes November's skies above
    and icy fields below?

Where do snowflakes come from?
I really want to know.
Who will shape a million jewels
 into a drift of snow?

Where do autumn nuts come from?
Do flowers fly away—
into a kingdom far away,
 until a summer day?

Where do winter trees come from,
Which drop their summer leaves?
And where do autumn colors go
 before November's freeze?

Where do cold winds blow from?
And why are they like that?
Is it because God turns down low
 his weather thermostat?

Where do winter birds come from?
And where do summer ones fly?
Does someone guide them on their way
on highways through the sky?

I know where winter comes from.
And where all summers go.
Each changing season comes from God.
He made the sun and snow.

December

What Shall I Give?

What shall I give to a friend
who has everything?
What shall I give that he doesn't have?
I could give him something
to keep him warm,
but keeping him warm would bring him
harm.
Do you know why?
No, that's not the best gift to give to my
friend.

What shall I give to a friend
who has everything?
What shall I give that he doesn't have?
I could give him something good to eat,
but he can't eat vegetables, soup, or
meat.
Do you know why?
No, that's not the best gift to give to my
friend.

What shall I give to a friend
who has everything?
What shall I give that he doesn't have?
I'll show him my room and offer a bed,
But he wants a snow pillow for his head.
Do you know why?
No, that's not the best gift to give to my
friend.

What shall I give to a friend
who has everything?
What shall I give that he doesn't have?
I'll send the best gift that I can—
to please my friend, a jolly SNOWMAN.
Now you know why!
It's the best gift of all,
for it's made just like him.

How Can I Make the Angels Sing?

How can I make the angels sing?
    What can I do or say?
If I help Mom and Dad
And try hard to obey,
Will that make the angels sing today?

SamB

How can I make the angels sing?
What can I do or say?
If I don't quarrel or fight
And am careful to do right,
Will that make
the angels
sing
today?

How can I
make the
angels
sing?
What
can I do
or say?
If I read in my
Bible
And I don't
forget to
pray,
Will that make
the angels
sing
today?

How can I make the angels sing?
What can I do or say?
If I help a friend know Jesus
And show him Jesus' way,
Will that make the angels sing today?

A Christmas Eve Gift

The moon was bright on Christmas Eve
  as Jeremy walked in the snow.
He smiled up and the moon smiled down.
He wished he could talk
  with the man in the moon,
and share some Christmas secrets.

"I wonder what gifts I'll get tonight,"
Jeremy whispered to himself.
He thought of the list he had given to
Dad,
and the copy he had given to Mom.
His list was as long as a kangaroo's tail
and he wanted everything on it.

There were gadgets and trinkets
and a cuddly bear,
and things to make and things to break.
There were candy canes and wind-up
trains
And things and things and things.
His list was as long as a kangaroo's tail
and he wanted everything on it.

Each step he took made him think of a
thing,
and each thing was bigger than
the thing before.
There were things enough
to crowd his room.
And things enough to squeeze out the
door.
Where, O where, would he put
all these things?
His list was as long as a kangaroo's tail,
and he wanted everything on it.

Jeremy thought the moon frowned
as he thought of those things.
Though the frown of the moon made him
frown a bit, too.

He couldn't stop thinking
of his list of things.
He couldn't stop thinking
of things he could make
and things he could run
and things he could hold.
Things and things, and things.
His list was as long as a kangaroo's tail
and he wanted everything on it.

Each step Jeremy took
said "crunch" in the snow.
He really wasn't sure
which way he would go.
But he wanted to walk
some more and think
of each thing he had put on his list.
He was sure he would get
every one, even more.
And the more he thought,
the more he wished
he had asked for more things
on his Christmas list.

But his list was already as long
as a kangaroo's tail,
and he wanted everything on it.

Then Jeremy stopped by a lamp
on the street,
a lamp wrapped with holly and snow.
He stood and looked
in the window nearby.
There he saw an old lady,
a lady alone in the soft yellow light,
a lady with no list and no one to love
on Christmas Eve.

A tear came to Jeremy's eye that night.
The lady alone
had no Christmas tree,
no gifts in the corner
wrapped in bright-colored paper,
no wreaths or cones or candy canes.
No children to sing and clap their
hands,
no laughter or feasting or fun.

What gift would she want?
And who would give it?
Then Jeremy thought
of the gifts on his list,
that list as long as a kangaroo's tail.
And he wasn't so sure he wanted each one.

Then Jeremy had a wonderful thought.
He ran home through the snow,
and up to his room.
In a wink and a twinkling
he was back once again.
He was back at the lamp
with the holly leaves.
He was back at the window
with soft yellow light.
He was back near the lady
with no gifts in sight.
He stood there with a book
in his hands on that night.

Jeremy lifted his book with a smile.

And he sang a sweet song
of the Christ Child's birth.
His song was a gift to the lady alone.
He smiled as he sang,
and she smiled, too.
Then he knew that his gift
was the best he could give.

In the snow that night,
by the soft yellow light,
Jeremy forgot the list he had made.
He forgot the list of things and things.
He was giving, not getting.
He was singing, not taking.
He was bringing a gift
of himself and his song.
And that was the best gift
on that Christmas Eve night.

There by the lamp as the snowflakes fell,
by the lamp with the holly leaves
wrapped all around,
Jeremy sang his songs of love.

He sang many songs of a Savior's birth

and the joy he could bring to a lady
alone.
Jeremy had a long list of songs to sing.
His list was as long as a kangaroo's tail
and he sang for her *every* one.

A Christmas Kitten

"What do you want for Christmas, Jody?" a friend asked.

"A kitty," said Jody. "I want a kitty to pet and call my own. I want to hear her purr. A kitty is soft and loving."

"I certainly hope you get one," said Jody's friend.

"What do you want for Christmas, Jody?" another friend asked.

"A kitty," said Jody. "I want a kitty so I can feed her and take care of her."

"I certainly hope you get one," said Jody's second friend.

"What do you want for Christmas, Jody?" a third friend asked.

"A kitty," said Jody. "I want a kitty to catch mice in my pony's barn. My dad says a kitty would be the best mouse catcher there is."

"I certainly hope you get one," said Jody's third friend.

When Jody got home on Christmas Eve, Mother put her arm around her and gave her a big hug. "You look like you swallowed a pickle," said Mother. "Or was it a lemon? Why so glum? Cheer up! It's the day before Christmas."

"I really do want a kitty for Christmas more than anything else," said Jody.

"I know you do," said Mother. "But I've already explained why you won't get one. I called the Humane Society and every pet shop around here. It seems that everyone wants a kitty this Christmas. There isn't one to be had. Unless something special happens, you must not expect a kitty for Christmas tomorrow."

Jody was very sad. No one likes to see little girls sad on Christmas Eve. Mother and Father didn't like it either. But what could they do about it?

That night Jody dreamed about a kitty. She dreamed that she was feeding the kitty. Then she dreamed that she was petting the kitty. Then she saw the kitty catching mice in her pony's barn. She was the best mouse catcher Jody had ever seen.

On Christmas morning Jody was excited about opening her gifts. She almost forgot about wanting a kitty as she opened each package. It really was a wonderful Christmas.

Jody had just finished opening her gifts when she heard the doorbell ring. "Will you see who's at the door, please?" Mother

Merry Christmas

asked Jody. "It may be someone who wants to see you."

Jody opened the door. She thought she would see one of her friends. But no one was there. Just then Jody heard a tiny noise. Something went "meeew."

Jody looked down and saw the most wonderful sight. There was a basket with six beautiful kitties in it.

Jody was so excited as she brought the basket into the house. "Are they really for me?" she asked Mother and Father.

"All six of them," said Mother. "Late last night Mrs. Brown down the street called. She asked if I knew anyone who would give a nice home to one of the kitties she had. I said I knew someone who would take good care of all six of them."

"Merry Christmas!" said Father.

What do you think Jody did the rest of the day?

Something Different for Christmas

Marsha giggled when she saw Andy playing in his room. It looked as if he was in a toy store. There were toys everywhere.

"You don't need any more toys for Christmas," said Marsha. "But what can I give you?"

"Something different," said Andy.

"Like what?" asked Marsha.

"Like something different from anything in this room," said Andy.

Just then Andy's dog Sandy looked into his room. "I suppose you'll ask what I want for Christmas, too," Andy grumbled at Sandy. Sandy just wagged his tail.

That night Marsha had a what-shall-we-get-Andy-for-Christmas meeting with Mother and Father. But no one knew what different gift Marsha could give him. "We'll just have to keep thinking about it, Marsha," Father said at last.

In the morning Marsha had a little talk with Sandy. Marsha did all the talking and Sandy wagged his tail. "I suppose you know exactly what to give Andy," she said. "I certainly don't."

Sandy wagged his tail again.

Then Marsha had a good idea. "Sandy, you and I will give Andy the most different gifts that he has ever had," she said. She could hardly wait until Christmas to give these different gifts to Andy.

On Christmas day Andy opened all his gifts. All but Marsha's gift. Where was that?

"Sandy and I have gifts for you outside," Marsha told Andy. "Come with us."

Andy put on his old coat and one of his Christmas hats and went with Marsha and Sandy. He was certainly surprised when Sandy gave Andy a bone with a ribbon on it. Then Andy saw a little note on the ribbon.

"My gift is the gift of Christmas happiness," said the note. "Give one of your special toys to a boy who doesn't have much. You will learn something about being happy." It was signed, "Sandy."

"Now let's go back in the house and put on the new coats and hats Grandma gave us," said Marsha. Andy didn't like to change clothes but this was Christmas and he was too happy to fuss over such a little chore.

"OK, now let's get my gift for you," said Marsha. She led Andy to a little ice cream stand.

"Usually I would charge you for this special snowball ice cream cone. But today it's free!" she said. "So is the Christmas note in the cone." When Andy ate the snowball, he found the little slip of paper in the cone.

"My gift is the gift of Christmas love," the note said. "Give one of your special toys to another boy who doesn't have much. You will learn something special about love." It was signed, "Marsha."

Andy thought about the two very different Christmas gifts. He thought about the Christ-

Pay
Here
ICE
CREAM
ANY FLAVOR
5¢
Red
Paint

mas happiness note and the Christmas love note.

"I'll do it!" he said.

Andy wrapped two special toys in Christmas paper. As he did, he felt happier than he had all day. "That's my gift of Christmas happiness," he said.

Then Andy thought of two boys at school who wouldn't get much for Christmas. He would take his special toys to them right now. Suddenly Andy felt more love in his heart than he had all day. "That's my gift of Christmas love," he said.

Soon Andy was walking down the street with the special Christmas toys. He was sure Marsha and Sandy had given him the very best Christmas gifts ever. What do you think?

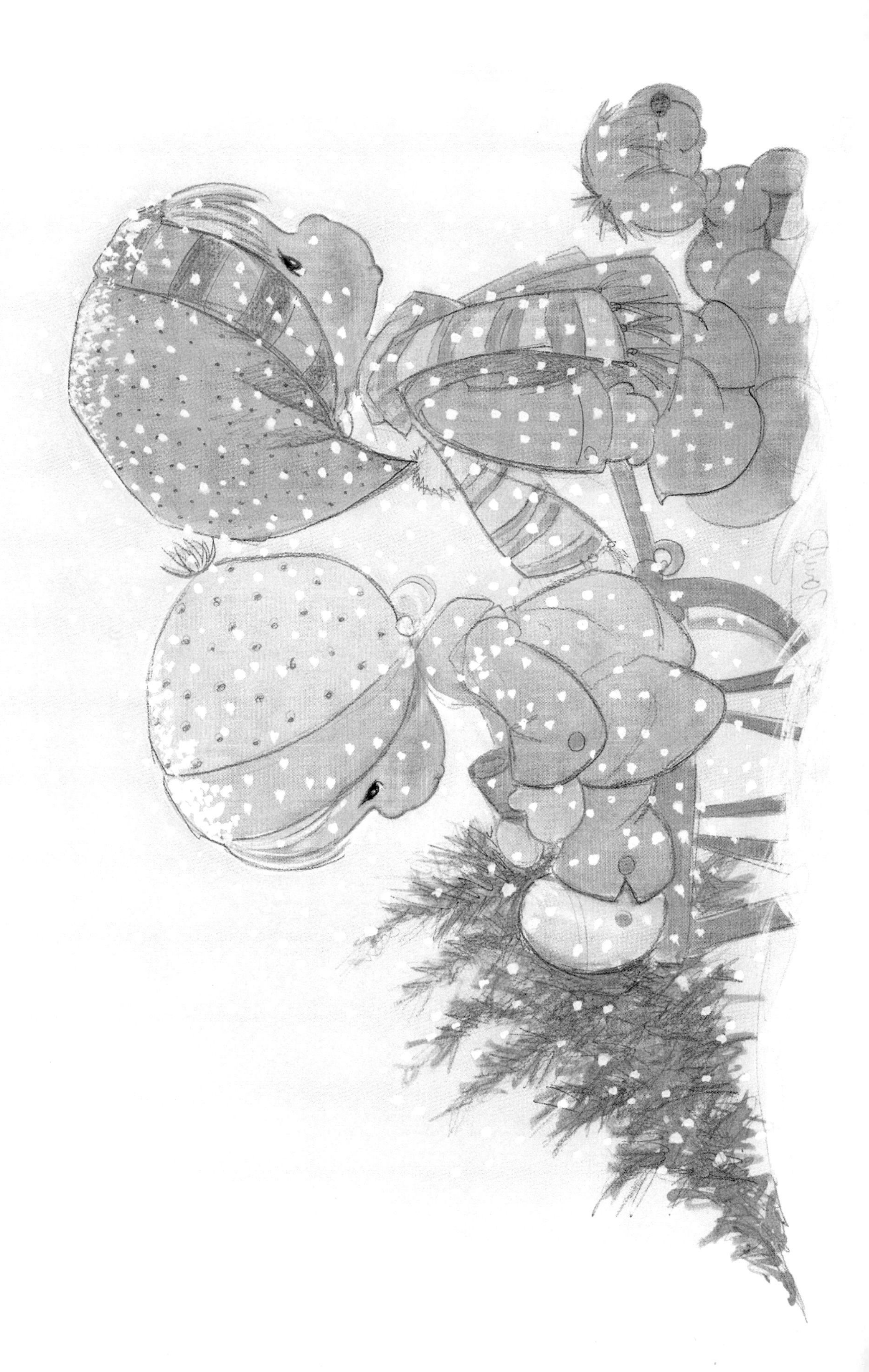